WALLY AND THE HOLIDAY JAILBREAK

ZACK THOUTT

Zack Thoutt: an imprint of Eudemonia 0x1 LLC

zackthoutt.com

Identifiers: ISBN 9781959745037 (paperback) | ISBN 9781959745044 (hardcover) | ISBN 9781959745020 (epub) | ISBN 9781959745068 (audiobook)

This is a work of fiction. Names, characters, places, and incidents either are the product of the author's imagination or are used fictitiously, and any resemblance to actual persons, living or dead, businesses, companies, events, or locales is entirely coincidental.

Contents

Parental Advisory

While *Wally and the Holiday Jailbreak* is told through the eyes of a third grader, it is an adult comedy that includes mature content. Parental discretion is advised.

While *Wally and the Holiday Jailbreak* is told through the eyes of a third grader, it is an adult comedy that includes mature content. Parental discretion is advised.

CHAPTER 1

THE TOILET CONUNDRUM

THREE SUCCESSIVE CHIMES rang over the Bear Creek Elementary School intercom like bells in the school Christmas choir. Two of Wally's classmates sprang to their feet and ran toward their backpacks, but Wally knew better. He glanced at his best friend, Sarah Evans, who was sitting on the edge of her red plastic seat with her elbows resting on her desk.

"Olivia, Charles, come sit back down," Mrs. Brenda said with her hands on her hips.

Mrs. Brenda wore a knee-length cotton dress covered in flowers and vines. Her short, voluminous brown hair was sculpted in place like a rock. Even the one time Mary flew off the swing and Mrs. Brenda had to run and save her, her hair never moved. Sarah's mom, Mrs. Evans, said it was because she used too much hairspray and that the smell gave her a headache, but Wally liked the smell.

"I won't see you for two weeks and two days. Does anyone know how many total days that is?" Mrs. Brenda asked.

Nobody raised their hand.

"Somebody must know... We can't start Christmas break until we know when to come back."

Wally knew the answer was sixteen days. He considered raising his hand, but the thought of it made his face turn hot. He didn't want everyone to look at him.

Kids from other classes were already throwing snowballs and making angels outside beyond the classroom windows. The snow was coming down hard enough that the mountains behind the school were no longer visible. Sarah's dad, Mr. Evans, told Sarah and Wally that Santa was making it snow for Christmas, but they had decided the week before that they didn't think Santa was real. Wally was worried that he didn't have a present for his father yet.

He scanned the room, hoping somebody else would tell Mrs. Brenda the answer. He had important shopping to do and needed to leave.

Sarah raised her hand. Black pigtails flowed from her round head down the back of her golden shirt with a glittery menorah on it. Her desk was on the other side of the classroom from Wally because Mrs. Brenda had caught them making eraser shavings for their collection the week before while she was talking and separated them.

"Sixteen," Sarah answered, "and it's holiday break, not Christmas break because some people don't celebrate Christmas."

"Very good, Sarah," Mrs. Brenda said, moving her hands

from resting on her hips to being clasped behind her back. "I will see you all in sixteen days. Have a Merry Christmas! You may go."

Most of the kids ran to pack their backpacks, but not Wally. He rushed over to Sarah.

He had found a white eraser on the floor in the hallway when he went to the bathroom after recess, and he spent all of history class rubbing it on a blank piece of paper, turning it into eraser shavings. He handed Sarah an empty metal mint tin full of the shavings.

Sarah opened the tin. "You found a white one?!" she exclaimed.

Wally nodded.

She ran back to her desk, raised the tabletop, and stacked the tin on top of three others inside. Most of their classmates were still bundling themselves in jackets, hats, and scarves when Wally's friend Jake sprinted toward the door on the opposite side of the classroom and shoved it open. Cold air rushed inside, blowing a cloud of snowflakes into the room. Jake was always the fastest to leave because his boots zipped up, so he didn't have to tie them.

Wally put his coat on, shoved his Minecraft lunchbox with a Creeper on it into his backpack, and tied the laces of his dirty white sneakers.

"Did your dad figure it out yet?" Sarah asked. Wally slung his backpack over his shoulders.

"Figure out what?" Olivia asked. She wore a pink jacket and gloves, and her ponytail protruded through a hole on the back of her purple beanie, which had an embroidered Olaf patch stitched to the front of it. Olivia's backpack was already on, and she was cradling a doll with long blonde hair and plastic skis clipped to her feet. Sarah and Olivia were friends, but Wally didn't like Olivia because all she ever wanted to do was play with dolls and convince Sarah to play too.

"Wally's dad is really sad because he can't figure out the meaning of life," Sarah told Olivia as she slid her arms into her jacket.

"My dad already knows that," Olivia replied.

The muscles between Wally's eyebrows twitched as he squeezed his backpack straps. His dad was a professor and way smarter than Olivia's dad. "No he doesn't," Wally countered.

Olivia nodded her head, "He told me."

Wally reached down and pulled Olivia's doll from her arms. One of its skis broke off and fell to the floor.

"Hey!" Olivia shouted, swiping at the air in the direction of the doll.

"Tell me," Wally demanded.

Olivia dropped her arms to her sides as her face scrunched up. She let out a wail like a baby, "Waaaahhhh!"

"Olivia, what's wrong?" Mrs. Brenda hollered from across the room.

Olivia stared at Wally, tears pouring down her face. Even though she was one of the first kids to turn nine years old in their class, she cried the most. That was another reason Wally didn't like her.

From the corner of his eye, Wally saw Mrs. Brenda take a step toward him. His heart raced in his chest at the thought of being sent to the principal's office. If he got in trouble, it would make his dad even sadder.

Olivia's sobs grew louder, "Ahhhhh!"

"Olivia, use your words," Mrs. Brenda demanded, marching toward them.

Olivia raised her arm and pointed at Wally. His stomach sank.

Wally glanced at Sarah, who was staring at him with an expressionless face. He dropped Olivia's doll, which landed on the ground next to its fallen ski. Wally thought about running straight out of the classroom and into Mr. Evans's car, but the door that exited directly outside was in the direction of both Olivia and Mrs. Brenda. Olivia fell to her knees to pick up her doll. Her face burned red like an apple as she screamed, "Nooooo!"

Wally turned around and slinked out of the other classroom door into the hallway with his head down, hoping Mrs. Brenda wouldn't notice him.

"Wally, come back here!" Mrs. Brenda yelled. She sounded mad. She'd never yelled at Wally like that before. He'd heard her yell at other kids, but never him.

Wally sprang into a sprint, almost tripping over his own feet. He hoped that Mrs. Brenda would stay back to help Olivia pick up her doll and that he'd have time to escape through the doors at the front of the school. If he could escape, she'd forget about what he did by the time they came back from holiday break. The halls were nearly empty, but a few older kids hugging textbooks against their chests stared at him as he flew past.

Wally glanced over his shoulder. His temples began pounding rapidly when he saw Mrs. Brenda burst through their classroom door. Her eyebrows were narrowed and the smile she usually wore all day long was turned upside down. He felt her eyes lock onto his back.

"Wally!" Mrs. Brenda shouted. "Stop!" She broke into a jog and followed him. He was pretty sure he could outrun her, but then he saw Principal Anderson and her long blonde hair emerge from her office at the other end of the hallway near the front doors of the school. She held her hand up as Wally approached. They had him surrounded.

Wally saw the boys' restroom on the right side of the hall. Mrs. Brenda and Principal Anderson were both girls and couldn't go into the boys' bathroom. If he could wait there until they left, he still had a shot to avoid trouble.

He barreled into the bathroom door, swinging it open, then stumbled into one of the stalls and locked the deadbolt. He climbed on top of the toilet and stood still while holding his breath.

The door creaked open. Its harsh sound echoing off the white tile floors reminded him of the horror movie Lenny's brother, Hunter, made them watch to scare them. "Wally, come out right now!" Mrs. Brenda commanded through the doorway.

Wally remained frozen. It sounded like Mrs. Brenda was waiting outside like he'd planned. For a moment he thought he was home free. Then he heard the clicks of Mrs. Brenda's heeled shoes tapping against the tile floor.

She couldn't come into the boys' bathroom! Jake went into

the girls' bathroom once, and Mrs. Brenda sent him to Principal Anderson's office. Wally jumped off the toilet and spun frantically looking for a way out.

Tap... Tap...

Mrs. Brenda's footsteps were getting closer. He wished he had to go to the bathroom. She couldn't come into the stall if he was using the bathroom. He'd tell on her if she did that. Not even a teacher was allowed to come in when somebody was using the bathroom.

Wally didn't have to go, though. He already went during lunch.

Tap... Tap...

Wally looked left and right. There was nowhere to run. He'd put himself in a cage. Maybe he could trick Mrs. Brenda into thinking he was using the bathroom? It was his only hope.

Wally leaned down toward the toilet. There were brown streak marks on the porcelain bowl and small bits of disintegrated toilet paper floating in the water. It smelled like after his dad used the toilet at their house.

Wally pressed his lips together, pushed air into his mouth inflating his cheeks, then squeezed the air out, making a fart noise with his mouth, "Pffffttt!"

Tap... Tap...

Why wasn't she stopping? He tried again, lowering his head closer to the toilet, "Pfffttt!"

Tap... Tap...

Mrs. Brenda must not have heard him. He needed to make the farts louder. Wally inhaled deep into his lungs, then pushed the air out his mouth with all his force. "Pffffffffttttttt!!!" The sound reverberated from inside the toilet bowl out into the restroom.

"Wally, unlock the door *right* now!" Mrs. Brenda demanded. She pushed on his stall's door. It was locked and didn't budge, so she shook it more violently. He could smell her hairspray.

Mrs. Brenda must not have believed he was actually using the toilet, otherwise she wouldn't try to come in. He needed something smelly he could put in the toilet so she'd believe he was pooping.

What was something smelly he could put in the toilet?

"Wally!" Mrs. Brenda shouted. "Come out right now. You're already in *big* trouble."

Mrs. Brenda had only yelled that loud twice all school year. Her sharp tone hurt his ears. His palms started sweating as he pulled his Creeper lunchbox from his backpack and unzipped it. His father made him a tuna sandwich every day even though he hated the smell of tuna. Mr. Evans usually gave him a better lunch when they picked him up for school and told Wally to throw the tuna away, but not to tell his dad because it would hurt his feelings. Wally was lucky he forgot to throw his tuna sandwich away that day. Now he had something smelly!

Wally opened the plastic bag. Chunks of pink meat were sandwiched between two pieces of white bread with the crusts cut off. He didn't know why his dad cut off the crust because he liked the crust. The smell of tuna made him gag, so he pulled the collar of his shirt over his nose and clamped his nostrils closed with his fingers.

Mrs. Brenda yelled at him again, "Wally!"

He ripped a piece of the sandwich off and dropped it into the toilet. It made a plunk sound when it hit the water. Just like a real turd! Surely this would trick her.

He almost forgot, "Pfffttt!"

"Wally, you're going to get a red card if you don't come out right now," Mrs. Brenda warned, shaking the door again.

He tore more pieces of the sandwich off and dropped them in the toilet. Plunk. Plunk. Plunk. "I'm pooping!" he shouted.

Plunk... Plunk... Plunk. "Pfffttt!"

The bread floated on top of the water with the old toilet paper, but the chunks of pink tuna sank slowly to the bottom of the bowl and covered some of the brown skid marks.

Wally's vision blurred as his eyes began to fill with tears. He didn't want to be in trouble before Christmas. He worried Santa wouldn't come and his dad wouldn't get his wish to figure out the meaning of life. Then he'd be sad for another year, and it would be Wally's fault.

"Pfffttt—" Wally made one more fart sound, but stopped halfway through when he started to cry.

"You have until the count of five to open this door," Mrs. Brenda demanded. "Five... Four... Three... Two..."

Wally reached for the door lock.

CHAPTER 2

THE RED CARD

WALLY SAT on a plastic chair hugging his backpack as Mrs. Brenda told Principal Anderson all the bad things he'd done. He didn't want to look at either of them, so he rested the right side of his face on the top of his backpack and thought about what he could get his father for Christmas.

His dad really liked coffee, but they already had five giant bags from Dunkin' Donuts stuffed into the cabinets above their refrigerator. Nothing came to mind except the meaning of life. It was the only thing his father said he wanted.

There were still four and a half days until Christmas. Wally didn't have much time, but if he could make it out of school without his dad finding out he got in trouble, he still had a shot at giving him a gift that would make him happy for Christmas.

Wally glanced out the window. Charlie and Miguel were building a snow fort as their parents talked, but almost everyone else had already left. Wally didn't see Sarah or Mr. Evans, who gave him a ride home every day.

Principal Anderson looked up at Mrs. Brenda from behind her desk and nodded her head. "I see, I've got it from here," she assured Mrs. Brenda.

Mrs. Brenda slammed Wally's bow and quiver of suction arrows onto Principal Anderson's desk. "You can also deal with this. He brought it to school on Monday and I haven't been able to get ahold of his father."

"I'll take care of it," Principal Anderson whispered. She winked at Wally as Mrs. Brenda turned around.

"Wally, have a Merry Christmas," Mrs. Brenda said with a huff. Wally didn't turn his head to acknowledge her.

The door clicking shut ushered in a torturous silence. Wally squirmed his legs in his chair. He felt trapped like he did in the bathroom stall. Jake told him Principal Anderson is nice, but Miguel told him that he had to see her once and she spanked his bare butt with a paddle, so he wasn't sure what to expect.

"Wally," Principal Anderson said. Her voice was soft. Wally glanced up and briefly met her gaze. Her face was smooth and her long, shiny blonde hair flowed around her ears. She scared Wally less than Mrs. Brenda, but he still closed his eyes and covered his face with his forearm when she asked him, "Can you tell me what happened?"

Mrs. Brenda had already told her what happened, so Wally didn't say anything...

Principal Anderson leaned forward and rested her elbows on the desk, "Is your dad outside?"

Wally looked up and shook his head with wide eyes. He

didn't want her to call his dad. He turned his neck to look outside for Mr. Evans again.

"Who are you looking for?" Principal Anderson asked.

"Sarah's dad," Wally replied.

The door swung back open, "Yes, Merry Christmas to you, too, Mrs. Brenda! Thanks for pointing me in the right direction," Mr. Evans hollered.

Mr. Evans was tall and skinny, and had a scruffy beard like a wizard. The hair on top of his head was just thin enough to catch glimpses of his scalp under the fluorescent lights, but thick, wiry hair sprang from the sides of his head like sections of a Slinky. Wally perked his head up when he saw Mr. Evans and felt an urge to run to him and hug his leg. He wanted to point out that he was still wearing sweatpants and that Mrs. Evans said none of them were allowed to wear sweats past ten in the morning. Then he remembered he was in trouble and dropped his head back onto his backpack.

"Hey, Bud," Mr. Evans said to Wally. He knelt down beside him and rested his hand on Wally's shoulder. "What happened?"

When Wally didn't say anything, Principal Anderson spoke up, "Apparently he stole a doll from his classmate, then ran from the teacher when he got caught."

"Is that true, Wally?" Mr. Evans asked.

Wally was crying now. He looked up at Mr. Evans and nodded his head, then smushed his face into his backpack.

"Whose doll?" Mr. Evans asked.

"A girl named Olivia," Principal Anderson replied.

Mr. Evans rose to his feet. "Sarah had her over to play a few weeks ago. She's very sensitive. Maybe there was a misunderstanding?"

"Sarah didn't see what happened?"

Mr. Evans shook his head. "She just told me Wally got in trouble."

"He won't tell me what happened, so I'm going to have to give him a red card," Principal Anderson said. Wally's heart rate jumped, his heart pounding rapidly against his chest. Nobody in his class had gotten a red card. They suspend you from school for one day, which Wally always thought sounded pleasant as far as punishments go, but he worried it would make his dad so sad, even the meaning of life wouldn't cheer him up. He curled back up and sobbed into his arms.

"Can I talk to you for a minute?" Mr. Evans asked.

Wally peeked through the gap between his forehead and arm to see Principal Anderson nod, then lean onto her desk and push herself to her feet. She was pregnant and had a big belly, so she waddled like a duck as she walked with Mr. Evans outside her office.

Wally heard whispers and made out some of their conversation, but not the whole thing.

"His dad..." he heard Mr. Evans say, "It's a difficult time at home..."

"...can't become a habit..."

"...practically lives at our house...some slack..."

"...you talk to him..."

The door opened.

"Wally, will you come out here?" Principal Anderson asked. "Grab your bow," she added.

Wally kept his backpack squeezed against his chest as he stood up and plodded toward them with his head down, grabbing his bow and quiver on the way.

"I'm going to let you off with a warning this time," Principal Anderson told him, "but that doesn't mean what you did today was OK. I want you to think about it over holiday break."

Wally nodded his head.

"OK, Bud, ready to leave?" Mr. Evans asked.

CHAPTER 3

THE SWEET BRIBE

SARAH'S DOG, Bee Bee, was sitting in Wally's seat when he opened the door to Mr. Evans's yellow Subaru. Bee Bee was a shaggy Bernese mountain dog with a head twice the size of Wally's. A small puddle of drool had pooled on the seat under her mouth. Bee Bee moved her head toward Wally and licked the air in his direction, but he recoiled.

Sarah tugged on Bee Bee's collar. "Bee Bee, watch out, Wally's afraid," she commanded from the middle seat. Bee Bee jumped down to the floorboard and rested her head in Sarah's lap. Wally threw his backpack over the seat, then plopped down as he pulled the door shut.

"Did you get in trouble?" Sarah asked.

Wally almost cried again as he replied softly, "Ya."

Sarah's younger sister, Eileen, extended her arm in front of Sarah's face and pointed at Wally. "Seatbelt," she told him.

Mr. Evans climbed into the car and let out an "Ahhh" as his

butt sank into the driver's seat. When he depressed the start button, the car turned on and hot air rushed through the vents. The stereo blasted a pop song through the speakers, "I came in like a wrecking ball!" Eileen sang along, "Ya, I just closed my eyes and swung!" Mr. Evans reached his arm toward the control panel and turned the volume down.

"Hey, that's my jam!" Eileen shouted. Her short blonde hair formed tight curls around her ears. She was wearing nothing but a diaper and was strapped into a pink booster seat like a race car driver. Her right hand clutched an empty purple sippy cup covered in glittery golden stars.

"We need to hear about Sarah and Wally's last day of school," Mr. Evans said. Eileen grunted as Mr. Evans put the car in drive and pulled out of the parking lot.

Mr. Evans looked at Wally and Sarah in the back seat through the rearview mirror. "How was the holiday party?" he asked.

"Mrs. Brenda kept calling it a Christmas party, and I corrected her like Mommy said," Sarah replied.

Eileen's face scrunched up. "I want Santa to come!" she complained.

"He's going to come, Sweetie. Plus, you just got to celebrate eight nights of Hanukkah and presents, remember?"

Eileen nodded and sucked at the teat of her empty sippy cup.

"How about you, Wally?" Mr. Evans asked.

Wally stared at Bee Bee, but he couldn't stop thinking about whether Mr. Evans would tell his dad about how he broke Olivia's toy, or if Principal Anderson had already called him. He didn't think Mr. Evans would tell on him because he was usually cool, but he might tell his dad about this. He wondered if Mr. Evans would get mad if he asked him to keep it secret.

Mr. Evans turned the radio off and decreased the flow of hot air blasting from the vents, "Wally, Bud, what happened?"

Sarah spoke up before Wally had a chance to respond, "Olivia told him her dad knows the meaning of life and wouldn't tell us!"

"The... What? What wouldn't she tell you?"

"Olivia said she knew and wouldn't tell us. She was keeping secrets and that's not nice."

Wally noticed Mr. Evans's gaze was directed at him in the rearview mirror and turned his head to avoid eye contact.

"Wait... What did she say she knew?" Mr. Evans asked.

"The meaning of life."

There was a pause. Wally held his breath, hoping Mr. Evans would change the subject. A blue pickup truck with dented and rusty doors flew past Wally's window, then cut in front of them. Mr. Evans accelerated to keep up.

"So, Wally, why did you take her doll?" Mr. Evans asked.

"He had to!" Sarah shouted. "She was lying!"

Mr. Evans bit his bottom lip as he cranked the steering wheel left. Wally slid into Sarah at the apex of the turn. When the car straightened out, Mr. Evans replied, "OK, well let's try not to take people's stuff even when they're mean, OK?"

"But she was keeping secrets and lying!" Sarah protested. "Mommy says we have to stand up for ourselves."

"Well, maybe next time you tell Olivia, 'I don't like that

you're lying and I don't want to speak with you anymore,' and you just leave it at that."

Mr. Evans made another sharp turn, then sped quickly up the street.

"To infinity, and beyond!" Eileen yelled.

Mr. Evans smiled and leaned his head to the left to see Eileen in the rearview mirror, "That's right, Sweetie."

"Do you know the meaning of life?" Sarah asked her dad.

"I... Why are you and Wally even wondering about that?" Mr. Evans asked.

"Because Wally's dad is really sad that he doesn't know, and we wanted to make him happy for Christmas," Sarah declared.

"Did he tell you that, Wally?" Mr. Evans asked.

Wally lifted his head from the cushion of his arms and nodded, "He was crying and when I asked him why, he said he couldn't figure out the meaning of life."

Mr. Evans took a deep breath and was silent for a minute. Wally felt Bee Bee panting hot air onto the back of his neck. He snapped back up to a seat and leaned onto the door away from Bee Bee.

"Do you know?" Sarah demanded.

"No, I'm sorry I don't know," Mr. Evans confessed, "But I think if we—"

"Does Mommy?" Sarah interrupted.

"No, I don't think she does, but you could ask her."

"Then who does?!"

"I think the only one who might know is Bee Bee."

"Bee Bee?!" Sarah exclaimed.

Wally crossed his arms and looked at Bee Bee, whose cheeks

were flapping against her teeth as hot air shot from the car vents onto her face.

Mr. Evans replied, "That's right, dogs know a lot about life that we don't."

Sarah grabbed both of Bee Bee's cheeks with her hands, "How do we make her tell us?"

Mr. Evans chuckled, "Well, she can't talk, so I guess you'll just have to watch her and see."

Wally wasn't sure if he believed Mr. Evans. He didn't think Mr. Evans would lie to them. He always told the truth and kept his promises, but this seemed unlikely.

"Are you going to tell my dad?" Wally murmured through a wavering voice.

Mr. Evans grinned at Wally in the rearview mirror and opened his mouth to reply, then abruptly shifted his attention back to the road as he slammed on the brakes. The car tires squealed against the pavement as they skidded to a stop and just avoided slamming into the blue truck. "It's green!" Mr. Evans complained, throwing his hand in the air.

"Just fucking go!" Eileen shouted.

Mr. Evans spun around, "Eileen, what did I tell you about saying that?!" There was a low grumble in his tone that perked up Wally's ears. Mr. Evans was never mad, but he was mad at Eileen. At least now Wally knew Mr. Evans wasn't mad at him earlier.

Sarah turned her head toward Wally and opened her mouth into the shape of an "O."

Eileen giggled uncontrollably.

"Eileen, you can't say that. I'm serious," Mr. Evans said.

"Did she just say the F word?" Sarah clarified.

"Sarah, don't start."

"Isn't she going to get in trouble?"

"She is in trouble," Mr. Evans asserted. He punched the accelerator and zoomed past a blue pickup truck.

Sarah protested, "If Wally got in trouble for taking Olivia's doll, then Eileen should get in twice as much trouble for saying the F word."

"Just fucking go!" Eileen shouted again.

"Eileen!" Mr. Evans yelled. "Santa doesn't bring presents to kids who use bad words. You're about to get put on the naughty list."

Eileen instantly opened her mouth and screamed as her face reddened. Her cries were so loud, Wally could feel them vibrating off the car windows. Bee Bee pushed her nose into Eileen's bare tummy, making her laugh a little between sobs, but Eileen didn't let herself become distracted. "Ahhh!" she cried.

"OK, you know what?" Mr. Evans hollered over Eileen. He swiped the turn signal into place, "Nobody's in trouble. Santa told me I could give each of you one free pass and you've used it—"

"But I didn't do any—" Sarah shouted, interrupting her dad.

"I don't care," Mr. Evans said. He turned into a parking lot. "You each used up your pass, and if you do anything else, Santa won't come. Understand?"

"Ahhh!" Eileen screamed. She threw her sippy cup at the back of the passenger seat. It bounced off the headrest and collided with Bee Bee's back. Sarah covered her ears with her hands.

"That's right. Eileen, if you say that word one more time, no Christmas presents," Mr. Evans declared. He pulled the car into a parking space and unbuckled his seatbelt, then leaned on the center console and turned to face them, "Now, what we're going to do is get ice cream and forget any of this happened."

Eileen's face was still scrunched and red, but she stopped crying. She looked confused. Wally was confused, too.

"Ice cream?" Sarah asked.

Wally looked out of the car window and saw a sign for "Sweet Cow Ice Cream" illuminated on the front of the building. Mr. Evans loved to take them there and he always got the biggest ice cream cone they had.

"That's right," Mr. Evans replied. "Here's the deal. Sarah, we forget what you and Wally did at school—"

Sarah spoke up again, "I didn't do—"

"Stop," Mr. Evans interrupted, pinching his fingers together in front of his face. "The deal is, we forget about all of it. We don't talk about it. Eileen, if you say those words ever again, Santa won't come. Sarah, stop arguing. Nobody says anything to Mommy. We all get a fresh start to holiday break. Can we make this deal?"

Wally looked at Sarah, who was taking an uncomfortably long time to respond. The free pass seemed like a no-brainer to him. "Deal," Wally replied. The knot in his stomach and tension in his neck eased as he unbuckled his seatbelt. Now he could focus on finding the meaning of life...after he ate his eggnog-flavored ice cream cone.

"Sarah? Eileen? We have to have a deal before we go in," Mr. Evans said, moving his gaze back and forth between the two of them.

"OK," Sarah replied, "but I didn't do anything."

"Eileen?" Mr. Evans asked.

Eileen nodded her head, "I want two scoops!"

Mr. Evans closed his eyes and sighed. "Just this one time," he said as he turned and exited the car.

Eileen wiped tears from her cheeks. "Ice cream!" she shouted jubilantly.

Wally swung the door open, almost hitting the white car next to them.

CHAPTER 4

THE VEGETARIAN

WALLY SAW SARAH'S blue house around the corner as they coasted down Northstar Court. They used to live close enough for Wally to ride his bike to their house, but moved at the start of the school year. Mr. Evans made Wally memorize their new address: 135 Northstar Court, Boulder, Colorado. He told Wally if anything ever happened to his dad, he should tell somebody to take him to their house.

Mountains of snow piled by plows covered the left side of the street. A large branch had fallen from a tree into the road ahead. Mr. Norris, Sarah's neighbor, was wrapping yellow caution tape around it when they pulled up. He wore knee-high white socks and cargo shorts. His long beard and white hair made him look like Santa, but Mr. Evans told them he was too grumpy to be Santa.

Mr. Norris stepped in front of the car and put his hand up as they approached. Mr. Evans pressed the brakes, which caused the car to slide to a stop on the snow-packed road. "What the hell are you doing?" he whispered to himself.

Mr. Norris walked around their car to the driver's side door and motioned for Mr. Evans to roll the window down.

As the glass lowered, letting cold air into the car, Mr. Norris bounced his finger up and down with it pointed at the ground. "How are you, Mr. Norris?" Mr. Evans asked.

A rainbow-colored wreath hung on Sarah's front door. The sun was setting and holiday decorations down the street switched on, one after another. Mr. Norris's house was across the street from Sarah's and his lawn was covered with illuminated plastic mannequins. Wally's favorite was the reindeer pulling Santa's sleigh. One of the reindeer had climbed on top of its friend's back, which Wally thought was strange.

"See what happened to my reindeer over there?" Mr. Norris asked, pointing at the reindeer laying on each other.

"The neighborhood kids messing with you again?"

Mr. Norris bent over and rested his hands on the bottom frame of the open window, "Do you know anything about it?"

"I'll keep an eye out, but I haven't seen anything."

"Mmhmm. We'll see," Mr. Norris replied. "Back when I first moved here many years ago, everyone on the entire street went all out decorating. Now the neighborhood's filled with so many Buddhists and Muslims and Hindus that it doesn't even feel like Christmas. Now I'm not saying anything's wrong with their beliefs, just that old Saint Nick should still be allowed his day to shine if they're gonna move here."

Sarah leaned over and whispered to Wally, "My mom and dad told me they hate Mr. Norris."

"Why?" Wally asked.

"My mom says he's really mean and we don't have to be nice to him because he's not nice to us."

"Maybe you can take it to the HOA," Mr. Evans replied to Mr. Norris.

"Don't think I haven't. You'll hear about it at the next board meeting. That and all the lazy people who can't even pick up after their dog. It's pathetic."

"Alright, looking forward to it," Mr. Evans said. He started rolling up the window, but Mr. Norris stuck his hand through the opening to stop him.

"Whoa there, one more thing. I'm going to leave some extra decorations on your driveway. I noticed you don't have many, so I thought I'd lend you some of mine. Maybe together we can make this section of the street look especially cheerful?"

"I'll try to find some time for it," Mr. Evans said. "I'm actually running late right now though." The car started moving slowly toward the Evanses' house.

Mr. Norris shuffled along with the car, "OK, I won't keep ya. If you get a moment to help me with this branch and contribute to the neighborhood, I'll be out here for the next hour or so."

"Sounds good, have a nice night, Mr. Norris."

Mr. Evans rolled up the window. "Freaking psycho," he complained as he pulled into the driveway.

Sarah's house was less decorated than Mr. Norris's, but they did have a single strand of red lights wrapped around the trunk of the big tree in their front yard. Snow in the driveway crunched and moaned as the car rolled to a stop. Wally exited the car as the garage door rose. A dozen bins of lights that hadn't been put up yet covered the space where Mr. Evans normally parked his car.

"Can we decorate?" Sarah pleaded.

"Daddy has his DnD stream, remember? I promise we can do it tomorrow," Mr. Evans said. He unbuckled Eileen from her seat and set her on the ground.

Sarah sulked as she hopped out of the car, "But that's what you said yesterday."

Mr. Evans glanced at his phone, then slid it back into his pocket. "Well, today you got ice cream."

Mr. Evans held Eileens hand as they shuffled past the bins. "I'm hungry!" Eileen shouted.

Mr. Evans opened the door to the house. "We just had ice cream."

"I want cereal."

"We're out of milk," Mr. Evans replied. He pulled his phone out again, then slid it back into his pocket. Bee Bee trotted inside and sat in front of her bowls, looking back at them over her shoulder.

Sarah and Wally followed Mr. Evans through the doorway, then Sarah dropped her backpack on top of a pile of shoes inside. "I want bagel bites," she said.

Wally set his backpack next to hers, removed his jacket and shoes, and placed them neatly where Sarah always put hers.

Mr. Evans surged into the kitchen, Sarah and Eileen following closely.

"I'm hungry!" Eileen complained.

"OK, fine, I'm making bagel bites," Mr. Evans said. He bent

over and yanked the freezer drawer open, rummaging through the bags and boxes to find bagel bites.

"I don't want bagel bites," Eileen declared.

"Uhh, Eileen, you're killing me. What *do* you want?"

"Fruity Pebbles."

"We don't have any milk... How about ribs?" Mr. Evans pulled a cardboard box from the freezer with a giant picture of a bagel-shaped pizza on it. The corners of the box were covered in ice.

Eileen thought about it for a moment, then nodded her head.

"Wally, are you hungry?" Mr. Evans asked.

Wally nodded his head, too. "I'll have bagel bites."

Mr. Evans dumped the entire box of bagel bites onto a white plate and shoved them into the microwave. Some of the frozen mini pizzas were upside down, but he didn't fix them.

Mr. Evans jogged to the refrigerator, pulled a Styrofoam box from the top shelf, then transferred three large rib bones covered in red meat to a plate. He opened the running microwave, slid Eileen's plate of ribs inside next to the plate of bagel bites, then pressed "Start" again. The plates collided with the walls, causing the tray to slide underneath.

"Dad, you have to make them up," Sarah complained.

"Sarah, I really don't have time for this." Mr. Evans checked his phone again, then jogged across the room and up the stairs. "I'll be right back!" he shouted.

Sarah's house was big. There was a large island in the kitchen, which opened out into the foyer and dining room on the left-hand side, and living room on the right-hand side.

There weren't many walls in their house compared to Wally's, and they had TVs everywhere. There was a giant TV in their living room above the brick fireplace that Wally had never seen turned on. Sarah always wanted to watch TV in her room. Bee Bee whined from the mud room, but Wally couldn't see her.

"How are we going to figure it out?" Sarah asked Wally.

Wally smiled. Sarah was good at solving mysteries and he knew finding the meaning of life would be one of the most challenging mysteries he'd ever tried to crack. "You want to know?" he asked.

"If it helps your dad."

Wally wasn't hungry anymore, he wanted to start collecting clues. "Your dad said only Bee Bee knows."

"He said all dogs know," Sarah clarified.

"But dogs can't talk."

"What do you think it looks like?"

Wally shrugged his shoulders, "I don't know."

"I don't understand what my dad wants, either," Sarah said.

"What does he want?"

"He wants to take my mom to Peru so she can get drunk."

Wally didn't know where Peru was, but he knew his dad wouldn't want to go there. He didn't like to go places.

Beep... Beep... Beeeeeep—the microwave timer went off. Mr. Evans ran down the stairs with a wooden staff in his hand, a brown cape running down his back, and a tall, pointy wizard hat atop his head.

"You shall not pass!" Eileen shouted at him.

"That's right, Sweetie, good job." Mr. Evans jogged toward the microwave, patting Eileen on the top of her head as he passed, then pulled the plates out and set them on the counter. Steam rose from the bagel bites emitting a familiar scent of herbs and bread that reminded Wally of being at the Evanses' house. Eileen's ribs sizzled and cracked on the plate even after they came out. Mr. Evans flicked them into a plastic bowl covered with the smiling faces of princesses. As he leaned over to set both dishes down on the kitchen table, one of the bagel bites slid off the plate onto the ground.

"Damn," Mr. Evans whispered. He dropped the plate and bowl on the table, then scurried over to the paper towel holder next to the kitchen sink, but only the cardboard core was left.

"Alexa," he shouted toward the black device on the kitchen island, "order more paper towels." Mr Evans bent down to pick up the fallen bagel bite with his hand, but Bee Bee swooped in and snatched it. She swallowed once, then looked up at him, panting and wagging her tail. "Uhhh," he grunted, "that will be fun later."

"What will?" Sarah asked.

Alexa spoke up. "I found an order from three weeks ago, 'Quick-size paper towels, 12 rolls.' Would you like me to reorder this?"

"Yes," Mr. Evans replied.

"What will be fun later, Daddy?" Sarah repeated.

Alexa interrupted Sarah again, "OK, your item should arrive on December 28th. Would you like to order anything else?"

"Jesus Christ," Mr. Evans exclaimed, looking down at his phone. "Sarah, make sure Eileen doesn't burn herself." He bent over Eileen, "Daddy has to do his stream. You eat up here with Sarah, then come down and see me when you're done, OK?"

Eileen nodded her head. Mr. Evans turned around and jogged in the other direction, this time descending down the stairs into the basement. Sarah pulled a chair out at the table for Eileen, who climbed onto it using both arms, then grabbed a rib with both hands and began ripping at the meat with her teeth. Sarah and Wally sat in chairs next to each other on the opposite side of the table with their bagel bites.

"I just had an idea..." Sarah said to Wally. "My dad says Alexa knows everything, too."

Wally turned around and eyed the device suspiciously. Meanwhile, Eileen's jaw was cranked wide open with her lips pressed against a meaty rib. Her mouth made sucking noises as she pulled down, ripping off flesh and exposing bright-white bone.

"Eileen, that's gross, Mommy says you can't make noises when you eat," Sarah told her sister.

Eileen held the bone in her mouth and stood up in her chair, hovering over the bowl of ribs. Bee Bee whined again from the mud room.

"Alexa, what's the meaning of life?" Sarah asked.

"According to Wikipedia, the meaning of life, or the answer to the question: 'What is the meaning of life?' pertains to the significance of living or existence in general. Many other related questions include: 'Why are we here?'; 'What is life all about?'; or 'What is the purpose of existence?' Does this answer your question?" Alexa replied in a monotone voice.

Sarah glanced at Wally. He didn't think it answered their

question, but he was confused. He decided to ask if she could help them find it, even if they didn't know what it was. "Alexa, where is the meaning of life?" Wally asked.

"According to Wikipedia, the meaning of life, as we perceive it, is derived from philosophical and religious contemplation of, and scientific inquiries about existence, social ties, consciousness, and happiness. Does this answer your question?"

"Alexa, order the meaning of life," Sarah commanded.

One of the rib bones was now completely clean of meat and Eileen was sucking on the end of it like it was the teat of her sippy cup. Bee Bee let out a low-pitched whine and barked, "Ruff!"

"I don't see that item in your purchase history, but I found some results that might be what you're looking for. Amazon's top choice is 'The Meaning of Life' by John Ritcher, fourteen dollars and ninety-nine cents. To order this item, just say, 'Buy it now.'"

"Buy it now," Sarah said.

"Ruff!" Bee Bee barked again.

"Your shipment will arrive after Christmas. You can upgrade to faster shipping for fifteen dollars and ninety-nine cents and receive your package by December twenty-fourth. Would you like to upgrade your shipping?"

"Yes," Sarah said.

"Your order has been placed. You can expect 'The Meaning of Life' to arrive by December twenty-fourth."

"What day is it," Sarah asked Wally.

"The twentieth," he replied.

There was a crash in the mud room, then Bee Bee trotted

into the kitchen with a ragged dragon toy in her mouth. Strands of frayed thread and clumps of brown stuffing hung from various holes on the red dragon. Eileen set the clean rib bone down on the table and picked up a second one, this time sucking even louder as she ripped the meat off. Her hands and face were covered in barbecue sauce.

"Do you think she'll send it to us?" Wally asked.

Sarah shrugged her shoulders again, "My dad uses it all the time and it works."

Alexa chimed in, "Are you done shopping?"

Bee Bee dropped the dragon toy at Eileens feet and lifted her nose toward the rib in Eileen's hand, sniffing furiously. Eileen stuck her elbow out and nudged Bee Bee in the face, but she persisted.

"Ehhh!" Eileen complained through her mouth full of meat.

"Bee Bee, bad!" Sarah shouted.

"I'm sorry, I didn't get that. Can you say it again?" Alexa responded.

Bee Bee climbed her front paws up onto the chair and reached her open mouth toward Eileen's face, then gently bit into the rib and pulled. "Ahh!" Eileen cried.

"Bee Bee, bad!" Sarah shouted again. "Bring the dragon!"

Bee Bee pulled the rib from Eileen's mouth and began licking it on the ground.

"Leave it, Bee Bee! Bad. Bring the dragon!" Sarah commanded.

Alexa spoke up, "I found an order from last week, 'Bad

Dragon Haiku dildo, large.' Would you like me to reorder this item?"

Sarah jumped down from her chair and grabbed Bee Bee's head in an armlock, "Wally, take it from her!"

"OK," Wally shouted. He slid off his chair and approached Bee Bee's giant head.

"I've reordered 'Bad Dragon Haiku dildo, large' for you. It will arrive with your other items on December 24th. You can ask me to check the shipping status," Alexa said.

Bee Bee whipped her head back and forth, avoiding Sarah's attempts to grab the rib. "Grab it!" Sarah called to Wally.

He extended his arm toward Bee Bee's face. Drool flung from her mouth onto Wally's hand and shirt as she squirmed to avoid his hand. Wally didn't have a dog and didn't know how to tell when one is going to bite you, so he grabbed onto the bone gently with just his pointer finger and thumb.

Sarah clenched Bee Bee's bottom jaw with her hand and attempted to pry her mouth open. "Take it from her!" she shouted.

"Is there anything else I can help you with," Alexa asked.

"No!" Eileen screamed, pointing at the rib in Bee Bee's mouth.

Wally pulled more forcefully at the rib, but Bee Bee didn't let go. The giant dog watched him from the corners of her eyes as drool oozed down both sides of her mouth. The rib was warm and slippery in Wally's fingers.

"OK, I'll be here if you need me," Alexa said.

Wally kept his grip on the rib bone, and turned his head toward the basement doorway when he heard the pounding of footsteps coming up the stairs. "What's going on up here!" Mr. Evans exclaimed. When Mr. Evans's head crested the edge of the staircase and he saw what was happening, he increased his pace and yelled, "Bee Bee, drop it!"

Bee Bee obeyed Mr. Evans and let go of the bone. The half-eaten rib rotated in Wally's fingers until it hung down, dripping with drool.

"My rib!" Eileen whined. She faced her belly to the edge of the chair and slid down to the ground, then ran over to Wally and yanked the rib out of his hand.

"Eileen, Sweetie, don't!" Mr. Evans tried to say, but it was too late.

Eileen stuck half the bone in her mouth and ripped most of the remaining meat off by yanking her head backwards. Mashing and breathing noises emanated from her mouth into an otherwise silent room as she chomped on the rib meat with her mouth hanging open.

Sarah turned toward Wally, "I think I want to be a vegetarian."

Eileen froze with her mouth full and looked at Mr. Evans. "I have to potty," she said.

"Then go to the bathroom," he replied, ushering Eileen forward with his hand on her back.

Eileen ran in the direction of the bathroom. "Bombs away!" she shouted.

CHAPTER 5

THE ADULT STUFF

WALLY TURNED the page of *The Boxcar Children: Mystery Ranch* and continued reading, "'Boy, look at that car!' said Benny, looking out the wa...window," Wally stuttered, sounding out the word. "It was long and low. It was pa...pa... painted yellow and black. A man got out of the car. A goo... a goo-ard?"

"What's a goo-ard?" Sarah asked.

They were laying on a pink bean bag under a blanket fort constructed of purple-striped white sheets and clothespins. Wally's right shoulder rested against Sarah's left as he held the book up to their faces. Sarah shined a flashlight on the book, illuminating both the page of the book and their fort.

Wally heard voices coming from downstairs and the sound of the front door opening.

"Is that your dad?" Sarah asked.

He heard the mumbles of his dad's voice, but couldn't make out any words. He closed the book and nodded at Sarah.

Wally pulled back the door of their fort and crawled out. Sarah's room was filled with furry pillows and pictures of dogs. Green glow-in-the-dark stars speckled her ceiling, lighting the room even after Sarah turned off the flashlight. Sarah followed Wally out of the fort, then clipped the door closed with a clothespin.

Wally dropped to his belly and crawled out of Sarah's bedroom to the staircase landing with Sarah in tow. He could hear what his dad and Mr. Evans were saying now that they were closer. Wally poked his head around the corner and gazed into the foyer through the railings at the top of the staircase. His dad looked sad as he stood on the blue and red rug just inside the Evanses' door. The chandelier hanging from the two-story ceiling shone light onto his balding head. The skin underneath his eyes sagged creating dark shadows on his face that contrasted his pale skin.

"What did the doctor say?" Mr. Evans asked. He was standing across from Wally's dad with his arms folded on his stomach. He still had his wizard cape on, but the pointy hat was resting on the edge of a coffee table in the living room.

Wally's dad bit his bottom lip and shook his head.

"Chemo?" Mr. Evans asked.

Wally's dad nodded. He looked like he was going to cry and wiped the bags under his eyes with his thumb.

Mr. Evans wrapped Wally's dad in a bear hug. His father buried his face into Mr. Evans's shoulder, his chest convulsing up and down as he sobbed.

"Why is your dad crying?" Sarah whispered.

Wally wasn't sure. Maybe his dad was sad that he couldn't find the meaning of life? Or maybe somebody had found it before him? He wanted his dad to be happy like Mr. Evans and wondered if Sarah did something for her dad that he didn't?

Mr. Evans pulled away, but kept his arm on Wally's dad's shoulder. "Let us know what you need," Mr. Evans said.

Wally's dad laid his head back and sighed, then wiped snot from below his nose with the back of his hand.

"Wally's welcome anytime," Mr. Evans said.

Wally's dad used his sleeve to dry his cheeks. "I'll need help next week. My first treatment's on Monday."

"You can drop him off on your way."

"They said I'll have side effects for forty-eight to seventy-two hours. Could he stay until Wednesday..." Wally's dad raised his voice to clarify, "I know it's Christmas Day. I just don't know how I'll feel."

"Of course. How about we drop him off Christmas morning so the two of you can spend the day together?"

Wally's dad pulled the zipper of his puffy jacket all the way up, then stuffed his hands into his pockets. It looked like he was shivering. "That'd be great, Sam... Thank you."

"Have you told work?" Mr. Evans asked.

Wally's dad shook his head. "I need to get this grant. I'm not tenured. If I don't get this grant..." he paused, "I don't know what... I already have bills showing up every day that I can hardly make sense of and the expensive stuff is just beginning."

Wally didn't want his dad to know they were spying, so he

crawled back to Sarah's room, stood up, then walked down the hallway to the staircase landing and waved.

"That makes sense," Wally heard Mr. Evans say as he walked around the corner and into earshot, "What about you? Can we—"

Wally's dad cut Mr. Evans off when he spotted Wally. "Hey, Bud," he called up the stairs.

"Sarah, why don't you help Wally put on his shoes and get his backpack," Mr. Evans said.

"Wally doesn't need help putting on his shoes," Sarah replied.

"Sarah, don't argue. Just do it."

Wally jogged down the stairs and across the kitchen toward the mud room. His socks slid across the hardwood floor and it kinda felt like he was ice skating. As he crossed into the mud room from the kitchen, he heard Mr. Evans resume their conversation.

"Did Mrs. Brenda call?" Mr. Evans asked quietly.

Wally's face flushed as his feet instantly came to a stop. Mr. Evans was breaking their deal. He didn't want to turn around and let them know he was listening, but he did want to hear what they were saying. Rather than go back, he froze facing the opposite direction and listened.

Wally's dad replied through a sigh, "She did."

That was it. His search for the meaning of life was going to end before it really began. Surely he'd be grounded for all of holiday break, and his dad wouldn't be happy on Christmas. What he did was bad.

Wally scurried into the mud room, rammed his feet into his

sneakers, then slipped his coat on. He knew his dad would ask about it on the car ride home. Even Mr. Evans said they should have been nice to Olivia when she was mean first, and Mr. Evans was the nicest dad Wally knew.

Wally tiptoed out of the mud room with his head down. "It was a misunderstanding," Mr. Evans told his dad. "The girl that told on him is challenging and I think they were all ready for a break."

Wally breathed a sigh of relief. Mr. Evans wasn't telling on him, he was making up a story to explain Mrs. Brenda's call. He knew Mr. Evans wouldn't break his promise.

Wally's dad opened his mouth to reply, but saw Wally had emerged and said to him, "You ready to go? I was thinking we could pick up pizza on the way home?"

Wally had already had bagel bites, but he still wanted pizza. He nodded, then hugged Sarah and Mr. Evans goodbye. Bee Bee followed him and pressed her nose up to his butt as he wrapped his arms around Mr. Evans. Wally squirmed to get away.

"No fart sniffing!" Eileen shouted at Bee Bee. Her sippy cup was now full of apple juice and she ran at Bee Bee pointing her finger.

"Gotcha," Mr. Evans said, picking Eileen up as she zoomed by.

When Wally left the Evanses' house, his father became quiet. They stepped carefully across the icy sidewalk to his green Subaru and hopped in. The window didn't roll up all the way and a frigid draft blew from the crack. Wally sat petrified in the back seat as his dad turned on the car and adjusted climate control to max heat. His dad hunched into a ball. His body shook as he slid mittens onto both hands. "Buckled up?" he asked through clattering teeth.

Wally nodded, anticipating his scolding that would surely follow. His dad yelled at him sometimes if he left the milk out on the counter after a bowl of Captain Crunch or if he lost one of his gloves at recess. He was prepared to be scolded ten times worse than that.

The car's starter whined as Wally's dad repeatedly turned the key in the ignition. When the engine finally started, it startled meekly to life. The smell of gasoline tickled Wally's nose.

Their car limped down the snow-packed streets in silence. When they made turns, the clicking of the blinker filled the void. Wally waited for his dad to bring up his call with Mrs. Brenda, the back of his throat periodically lurching up like it wanted to jump from his mouth.

What felt like an entire school day passed before Wally's dad parked the car in front of Cosmos Pizza and turned off the ignition. He looked at Wally in the rearview mirror and smiled. "The usual?" he asked.

"With chipotle ranch," Wally muttered.

Wally watched students in short dresses and sweaters stumble into Cosmos, unable to walk straight without holding each other up. His dad looked like a statue inside the restaurant compared to the constant motion of the college kids leaning back in their chairs laughing and throwing their hands about as they talked.

Wally's stomach growled when his dad started marching

toward the car, each of his hands holding a white paper plate with a giant slice of pizza on it.

His dad slid back into the car. "We got the last two cheese slices," he said. "Why don't you come into the front seat while we eat?"

Wally unbuckled himself and climbed over the car console into the passenger seat. His dad handed him a paper plate with both a slice of pizza and a portion cup full of chipotle ranch, then pulled two Mountain Dews from his jacket pocket and cracked them open.

They ate mostly in silence. When Wally looked up at his dad a few times and smiled, he smiled back. The tension in Wally's stomach relaxed as he sunk his teeth into the warm cheesy pizza. Mr. Evans had kept his promise and made sure he didn't get in trouble.

After Wally's dad finished his last bite of crust, he tipped his soda can into the air and chugged the remainder of it, then wiped his mouth with a napkin covered in orange grease stains. "I've got something to tell you, Bud," he said. His voice was quiet and solemn.

Wally's eyes started to water. He was scared, though he didn't know why.

"I'm not going to be around as much for a while. I'll be back... But you're going to hang out with Sarah and Mr. Evans more. Is that OK?"

Wally felt tears fall from his eyes. He didn't want to cry, but he was. He nodded his head at his dad.

"There's no reason to be scared," his dad said, wiping tears from his cheeks. "I've just got to work and then I'll be back."

"Can I help?" Wally asked.

"I wish you could. I really do. But this is adult stuff."

"Are you looking for the meaning of life?"

"I—" His dad chuckled, "Yep. That's right, Bud. I've just gotta figure a few things out." Wally's dad leaned over the center console and wrapped him in a hug. He smelled like pizza and dust bunnies. "I love you so much, Buddy." Wally cried as he hugged his dad back.

CHAPTER 6

THE BLUE SCREEN

WALLY WOKE up as the sun was rising on Sunday morning. Condensation dripped down the icy window next to his bed. Something was rustling in the branches of the tree outside, though he could not see what. His dad liked to sleep in on the weekends and got mad at Wally if he was noisy and woke him up, so Wally lay in bed thinking about how he and Sarah would find the meaning of life.

Alexa was a promising lead, but they still had to wait several more days to see what she sent. Wally was suspicious that she wouldn't give them what his dad wanted. His father hated Amazon and said he preferred to go to a store to buy things. If she didn't deliver the meaning of life, their best option would be to ask Bee Bee like Mr. Evans had told them to do.

Wally thought more about why his dad wanted to know the meaning of life. Mr. Evans didn't know, and he was happy. He decided that didn't matter, though. His dad had one item on his Christmas list and Wally needed to get it for him.

A few days earlier, Wally's father had told him the reason he never had time to play was that he had to work and take care of him, which was two jobs. Sarah's parents each only did one job and that was why Mr. Evans had time to make food and play video games with them.

Wally thought his dad was saying he wanted a mom for him, so he asked what happened to his mom. His father had told him she died when he was a baby.

By the time the sun melted the ice off the window, revealing the snowscaped park outside, Wally's stomach was growling. The sound of his father's grumbling snores vibrated the wall their rooms shared. Wally didn't want to wait longer for breakfast, so he inched the door open and tiptoed down the hallway of their apartment.

Whenever he stayed the night at Sarah's house on the weekends, Mr. Evans made them something special for breakfast. "Sunday is waffle day," he always told them, "and they're only good if you make them from scratch."

Wally felt like waffles, so he pushed one of the wooden kitchen chairs to the refrigerator, climbed on top, and pulled a box of frozen waffles out of the freezer. The toaster oven was off limits unless his dad was in the room. Wally didn't want to eat frozen waffles, though, so he slid three in and set the timer for three minutes. As the pale dough slowly thawed and cooked to a crispy golden brown color, Wally wondered if he and Sarah would find the meaning of life for his dad. He glanced at the Christmas tree. There were no presents or decorations yet.

When the toaster oven timer dinged, he used a fork to slide them onto a plate. Their warm, sweet scent rose into his face as he carried his plate to the table. Mr. Evans told them waffles were best with butter and maple syrup, so he searched the fridge for those toppings. He found a yellow tub of margarine and a bottle of Mrs. Butterworth's Syrup. The slab of margarine he plopped onto each waffle melted quickly and was dispersed throughout the wells of the waffle by generous pours of thick syrup.

Wally sat down at the kitchen table and ate the waffles with his hands. They were good, but not as good as the ones Mr. Evans made. He looked out their kitchen window. Sometimes, during the previous summer, a green hummingbird had visited in the mornings. He hadn't seen that bird for several months, though.

Wally's father emerged from the hallway as Wally was swallowing his last bite of food. He stuck each finger into his mouth and licked off the syrup and margarine that had dripped onto his hands as he observed his father. He looked pale, almost ghostlike. His gray sweatpants and matching sweater sagged on his boney shoulders. His face was almost expressionless.

"Want any waffles?" Wally asked.

His father walked past him, "No thanks, Buddy, I'll stick with coffee." He tripped on his own foot when he stepped off the living room carpet into the tiled kitchen, but caught himself on the countertop and didn't appear to be fazed. Seconds later, steaming liquid flowed from the coffee maker's glass pitcher into a big white mug with a buffalo on it. Wally watched as his dad stumbled first to the coat rack and slipped on his beanie, then to his work desk.

Stacks of paper covered all of the desktop except where the computer's mouse and keyboard rested. His father's fingers tapped a few keys until the monitor lit up. He took a sip of coffee as he scrolled with his right hand on the mouse.

Wally thought his dad looked sad again. He had an idea that it might be fun to play together, so he walked up to his father and tapped him on the arm.

"Mhmm?" his father responded without looking at him. He was sitting hunched toward the computer, the blue light of the screen reflecting off his glasses.

"Wanna play a game?" he asked.

"I can't right now."

"Do you need help?"

"Not right now, this is adult stuff."

Wally noticed his bow and arrow resting against the wall near the front door. "What about hunting?"

"I'd love to, Bud, but I really need to work so we can hangout on Christmas. How about you go outside and scout with your bow? We can go in a couple days."

When Wally headed toward the coat rack to bundle up before venturing outside, his father called without taking his eyes off his computer, "Put your dish in the sink."

Wally did as his father asked, then got dressed and headed downstairs. He slung the quiver across his back and he held his bow with an arrow nocked, ready to let it fly at any squirrel he might see.

Wind was howling through the tree branches and enough

snow was being whipped up that visibility was obscured. A target made out of an old whiteboard with a bullseye on it hung from the tree he could see out his bedroom window. He took a few warm-up shots. On the first shot, the wind blew his arrow to the right, missing both the tree and target altogether. His second and third shots hit the target, the second one sticking particularly close to the bullseye. Wally pulled both suction-tipped arrows from the whiteboard with a pop, then dug his first arrow from the snow and put it back into his quiver.

Wally knew a squirrel lived in the tree on the other side of the path that ran between their apartment and the park. He slid behind a bush growing against the building and crouched to hide.

A sequence of gusts bashed into Wally's exposed face as he sat waiting for the squirrel. The only sounds were the wind rushing across his ears and tree branches creaking overhead. When his mind drifted off into thought again, an idea sprang into his head—maybe the meaning of life was a new mom. If that were true, it would make sense why his dad was so sad. Sometimes he felt sad that he didn't have a mom, too.

A few minutes later, a squirrel scurried down the tree he was watching and hopped onto the top of the crusted snow. Wally noticed a girl wearing yoga pants and a big pink puffy jacket walking toward him down the sidewalk as he pulled the arrow back. She was staring at her phone scrolling repeatedly with her thumb. Wally took aim at the squirrel as the girl entered the path his arrow would travel in. When the squirrel turned and ran back up the tree, he decided to let the arrow fly.

The arrow sailed within inches of the girl's face, though she didn't notice. Wally thought it was going to hit the squirrel right in the ribs, then a gust of wind pushed it to the right at the last second. The arrow lodged itself in a few of the lower branches.

Wally stood up to retrieve his arrow, but paused when he heard the squirrel chirping angrily. The squirrel stood up on one of the branches and chucked a nut at the girl walking down the path, hitting her in the face.

She dropped her phone and ran down the path screaming, then stopped when she heard the squirrel chirping. She walked back toward the squirrel covering her eye with one of her hands, recovered her phone, then resumed walking down the path.

When Wally saw the squirrel grab for his arrow, he stumbled out of the bush and ran toward the tree. The squirrel pulled the arrow into the higher branches as Wally approached and jumped at the furry critter without success. The arrow was out of reach.

He was down to two arrows and hoped Santa would bring him more in a few days. He wondered what Sarah was doing and if she'd found the meaning of life yet.

CHAPTER 7

THE YARN BALL

WALLY WOKE up just after sunrise again the next morning and was surprised to hear his dad rummaging in the kitchen. He got dressed and emerged from his bedroom, excited to go to Sarah's house.

"I was about to wake you up. You ready to go?"

Wally nodded his head. Lately his father moved slowly and talked slowly too, but this morning he was jolty and barely paused between words.

"Alright, come put your shoes on."

Wally's father paced back and forth between the front door and the kitchen, stopping to take occasional sips of his coffee. Wally put his hat and coat on, then dropped to the floor and tied his sneakers.

When he stood up with all of his gear on, his father crouched down and brushed Wally's hair across his forehead.

His hands were shaking. "You sure you're going to be OK at the Evanses' house?"

"Ya," Wally replied. Something in his father's voice made him feel like crying again, but he did his best to hold back tears.

"I love you so much, Wally. Don't ever forget that." His father pulled him into a hug. Wally squeezed him as tears fell down his cheek. He didn't know why his dad kept hugging him like this, but it scared him.

His father wiped his nose as he stood up, "Alright, let's go." He pointed at the wall near the coat rack, "Don't forget your bow," he said.

Wally grabbed his bow and quiver, then followed his father into the hallway. The smell of bacon wafted down the hall from someone else's unit.

Wally's father didn't say anything on the rest of their journey to Sarah's house. He drove faster than normal and his hands shook on the steering wheel. Wally rang the doorbell and stood with his nose inches away from the door, but backed up when he heard Bee Bee's deep bark and her claws sliding across the hardwood floor.

Wally's father seemed to relax as he chatted with Mr. Evans just inside their house. Sarah stood by her father with her hands behind her back, waiting for the grownups to finish.

The air smelled like stewing meat and vegetables. Wally peered into the kitchen and smiled when he saw a crockpot sitting on the counter. Mr. Evans always made the best food.

"I'll be back in two days," Wally's dad told him when he finally turned around. He crouched down to Wally's height and held his shoulders. His hands weren't shaking anymore.

"For Christmas, right?" Wally clarified.

"Ya, I'll pick you up Christmas morning after I make sure Santa makes it home safe."

His dad stood up. "Are we dropping him off?" Mr. Evans asked.

"No, it'll be nice to get out of the house."

"Let us know how you're feeling. You sure you don't want a ride home later today? Some food?"

"Ya, Larry down the hall is coming with me. Taking care of Wally is a huge help."

"OK. Let us know how you're doing."

Wally's dad casually wrapped one arm around Mr. Evans and patted him on the back, "Hey, are you still DMing that Christmas one shot?"

"Yes," Mr. Evans replied. He sounded surprised, "You wanna play?"

"Is there room for a bard in the group?"

"Yes, it'll be nice to have you back like old times! If you have the energy tomorrow, send your character sheet. We're starting at level five."

"Alright, count me in." Wally's dad waved as he stepped through the front door.

Sarah tugged on Wally's shirt sleeve as his dad pulled out of the driveway and coasted down the street. "Guess what?!" she asked.

Wally was caught off guard and paused to think, "...Did your mom get us more clips for our fort?"

"No, she's not home yet. I saw Lenny riding bikes and he told me you could have his new talking dog."

Wally didn't know what to say. "I don't want a dog," is what came out. His dad told him dogs were too expensive and that they didn't have time to care for one. Sometimes he was also scared they would bite him. He knew he couldn't bring a dog home.

"But how else are you going to find out?" Sarah asked.

"Out what?" Wally replied.

"The meaning of life. Lenny's dog can tell us," she said.

"Dogs can't talk."

Sarah's eyes narrowed, "I think they can."

"Bee Bee won't talk."

"She's dumb. My dad says she fell off a turnip truck."

Wally still wasn't sure if he believed her. "What about Alexa?" he asked.

"I asked her this morning and she said it would be here tomorrow. Let's go to Lenny's and see."

Wally still had his sneakers, jacket, and hat on. He stood near the door while Sarah ran to the mudroom and put her winter gear on. He didn't want to meet another dog, but Sarah seemed determined to go. Bee Bee tried to approach Wally, but he backed up until his butt hit the front door. He held both hands at arm's length in the direction of Bee Bee's face as she sniffed the air and wagged her tail.

"Bee Bee, let's give Wally some space," Mr. Evans said. He grabbed her collar and ushered her across the room in the direction of the basement. "Did I hear you're going to Lenny's?" he called to Sarah.

"Yes," Sarah replied, "and we don't need help."

"I want you back in one hour. It's eleven o'clock now, that means you have to be home at noon. Understand?"

"Yes!" Sarah yelled. She stomped through the living room and flung the front door open, its handle smashing into the wall. Wally followed her outside.

Mr. Evans hollered as Sarah marched down the front steps, "Use the path and don't cross the street!"

"OK!" she screamed.

Wally waved goodbye and realized that they forgot to close the door. Mr. Evans got mad once when they left the door open and Bee Bee got out, so Wally ran back and shut it. The sun was shining onto the snow that had fallen the day before. Most of it was still white and fresh. Sarah made a snowball and chucked it at her dad's car. It smashed into the front passenger window leaving a snow splatter. Then she marched across the street without looking back.

"Aren't we taking the path?" Wally asked Sarah from the edge of the driveway.

"I'm not a little kid," she replied.

Wally looked both ways for cars and turned around to check the door and windows for Mr. Evans. The coast was clear. He took a deep breath, then sprinted past Sarah to the other side of the street.

Wally had forgotten his gloves in his dad's car and his hands were freezing. Sarah seethed silently with her face scrunched. When they arrived at Lenny's house two and a half blocks later, she marched straight to the front door and rang the doorbell three times in a row, which made Wally feel uncomfortable.

Lenny's brother, Hunter, swung the door wide open. His hair was pitch black and swooped over the top of his head, running down the left side of his face to his neck. He had a long, angular face with rainbow studs in his ears. Hunter was four years older than them and a middle schooler.

Sometimes when Lenny's oldest brother, Jason, babysat Wally, Sarah, and Lenny, Hunter would try to make them do things they didn't want to do. Last time their parents went to dinner, Hunter made Wally go through his haunted house and chased him with a flaming bottle of Axe Body Spray. Wally took a step back from the door.

Hunter pointed his pink-painted fingernail at Sarah and asked, "What do you want?"

"We're here to take your dog," Sarah replied.

Hunter dropped his voice to make it deep and rumbly like an evil lord, "Well you will never get him. Muhahahahah!"

Sarah turned around and gave Wally a look of bitter frustration. Then she declared, "Lenny said we could have him."

Hunter leaned his head back and raised his arms to the sky. "The only way to achieve your lofty goal is to face the horrors of my Dungeon of Peril. Muhaha!"

As Hunter was simulating the dimming echo of his evil laugh, Sarah squatted to the ground, picked up a ball of snow with her right hand, then pulled the elastic of Hunter's sweatpants and shoved the snow into his underwear.

"What the—" Hunter flailed. He swatted Sarah's arms away before she could recoil them, then bent over and shoved his hands into his pants as he made high-pitched girl sounds, "Ahh! Ahh!"

Sarah marched past him and into the house. Wally didn't want to be alone with Hunter when he recovered, so he slipped by and followed Sarah up the stairs toward Lenny's room.

As they approached the top of the stairs, Wally heard two bangs against the walls. Then a white and black puppy bolted into view at the top of the stairs. He was carrying a giant ball of yarn, which was unraveling behind him. The dog tossed the ball of yarn into the air. It landed on the first step, then tumbled down the stairs. Wally jumped out of the way as it rolled past him and onto the staircase landing, where Hunter was still scooping snow from his pants.

"That's him. Grab him!" Sarah commanded.

The dog lunged down the stairs after the yarn ball. Sarah tried to grab his collar, but he slipped from her grip. Wally bent toward the dog to catch him, but backed up against the railing at the last minute and let the dog run by.

"Bop, stop!" Lenny shouted from down the hall. He ran around the corner and froze when he saw Sarah and Wally. "What are you doing here?" he asked.

"We've come for the talking dog," Sarah replied.

Wally watched the dog zoom back and forth from room to room. Yarn was tangling around the legs of couches, tables, and chairs, forming a web throughout the downstairs level of the house.

"Don't let him get out," Lenny called from upstairs.

Wally noticed he had left the door open when he came inside! Hunter's normally pale face was red. Wally couldn't tell if he was mad or about to cry until he spoke, "Bop, come back here!" There was no more playfulness in his voice. Hunter picked up a pillow from the couch and chucked it at Bop, hitting him in the butt, though Bop was unfazed. "I hate you, damn dog," he muttered to himself.

Bop had unrolled the entire ball of yarn and started tugging on the end of it, which caused a table in the living room to tip over. A lamp shattered when it hit the floor and a bowl scattered Hershey's Kisses all over the ground.

"He can't have chocolate," Lenny said as he barreled past Wally down the stairs.

Bop sauntered over to the chocolate graveyard wagging his tail and sniffing. Hunter reached for his collar, but Bop saw him coming and evaded his grab. Lenny circled around to the other side of Bop, and slowly, the two brothers closed in on him.

"Sit. Sit," Hunter commanded. "Sit."

Bop put his ears back and sat. His tail brushed back and forth, sweeping foil-covered chocolates across the ground. Hunter bent down slowly, reaching his arms toward Bop. Just as he was about to grab him, Bop sprang to his feet and launched himself out the front door. The dog leaped off the porch and bounded through snow in the front yard like Wally had seen deer do at Sarah's house.

"We have to get him!" Lenny shouted.

Lenny and Hunter ran out of the front door barefoot, but stopped in their tracks when they reached the edge of the covered porch, which dropped off into several feet of powdery snow. Wally followed when Sarah ran down the stairs.

"Come, Bop. Come!" Lenny hollered.

Bop turned to face them in the front yard with his butt in the air and tail wagging. "Ruff. Ruff," he barked at them.

Sarah ran through the doorway. "Grab Bop's leash," she hollered to Wally, pointing at a green leash hanging from a coat rack.

The hook was too tall for Wally, so when he pulled on the leash, the entire coat rack crashed to the ground.

Sarah darted past Lenny and into the yard after Bop. The dog juked both left and right as she approached, but Sarah wasn't fazed. She jumped at Bop like she was diving into a pool. Both her feet rose into the air until her body was horizontal. For a moment, it looked like she was going to land right on Bop and tackle him, then Bop jolted backward at the last second. Sarah's face disappeared into a tall drift of snow. Bop barked again, then started running in circles around Sarah with his butt tucked under.

"Sarah!" Wally yelled. Her torso was planted upside down into the snow with her feet kicking in the air above. Wally sprinted outside to help her. When his right foot landed on a sheet of hidden ice, he slipped backward and fell, his head colliding with the last wooden stair of the porch.

Wally's world spun and went bright. He heard lots of yelling and barking. Then someone was hovering over his face. He felt warm air blowing over his nose. It tickled. As his vision came into focus, he saw Bop's snout hovering a few inches from his face dripping snot onto his lips. His front fangs looked long and sharp.

Wally briefly creaked his eyes open and met Bop's gaze, sure that he was about to be eaten, but scrunched them shut when the dog began sniffing his face and ears. When Wally felt a warm sensation moving across his cheek, he was sure his time was up.

It felt like someone was wiping a warm, wet towel across his face. He was surprised that being eaten didn't feel more painful, but he'd never been bitten before and didn't know what it was supposed to feel like. "No," Wally yelled. "Ahh!" He moved his hands up to cover his face and pushed at Bop's neck, which only made the dog lean into Wally more. "Help. Help!" Wally shouted.

"Good boy, Bop," Wally heard Sarah say.

Bop hopped off Wally and turned around to wag his tail at Sarah as she approached. Wally's hands shot to his face to assess the damage. His skin felt wet. Was that blood?

"Wally, are you OK?" Sarah asked. She grabbed Bop's collar and bent over Wally.

"I don't know," Wally replied.

Bop sat down in the snow beside Wally. He eyed the dog suspiciously.

"You saved Bop! He's never given me kisses," Lenny said from the edge of the porch.

Were those kisses? Wally wasn't sure. "Did he bite me?" Wally asked, still brushing his cold fingers across his face.

Sarah started laughing, "No, he was kissing you because he knew you were hurt. I told you, dogs know everything."

With the clarity of hindsight, Bop's kisses were kinda nice. Wally rose to a seat on the ground. Bop put his ears back and whined at Wally.

"You should tell him he's a good boy," Sarah told Wally.

Wally tentatively reached his hand toward Bop's head. His tail wagged furiously back and forth, creating a cloud of powdery snow behind him. "Good boy," Wally said, stroking Bop's head. Bop closed his eyes and leaned into Wally's pets.

Wally was still holding Bop's leash with his other hand. Sarah grabbed the end of the leash and clipped it to Bop's collar.

Hunter stomped down the porch stairs. He'd put on a pair of leather cowboy boots, which made loud thuds with each step. "Give me our dog!" Hunter shouted as he reached for Bop's leash.

Wally yanked the leash away from Hunter's swipe, but he wasn't fast enough. Hunter grabbed on and pulled.

"Get away," Sarah said. She picked up a snowball and chucked it at Hunter's face.

"Ahh!" Hunter groaned. He yanked back and forth on the leash, pulling Wally onto his stomach. "Let go," he commanded.

The leash was wrapped around Wally's wrist and he couldn't let go even if he wanted to. Hunter dragged Wally through the snow toward their house. The leash loop burned and contorted Wally's arm as he struggled to slip free. "Ow, that hurts," Wally cried.

Lenny yelled at Hunter from the porch, "Stop! You're gonna hurt him."

"He's our dog," Hunter spat back. "Let go." Hunter paused and kicked Wally in the stomach with the tip of his cowboy boot. Wally curled into a ball and grunted. He tried to pull his hand free, but it was still stuck in the leash loop. Hunter kicked him again, this time in the back.

Wally heard a growl, then felt the breeze of Bop jumping over him in the direction of Hunter. He peeked his eyes through his arms and saw Bop showing his teeth to Hunter. "Bark. Bark."

Hunter yanked on the leash again, this time pulling hard enough to rip it off Wally's wrist. Then Hunter yanked on the leash a second time, whipping Bop's neck. Bop lunged toward Hunter, snarling, and bit his hand.

"Ouch!" Hunter exclaimed, dropping the leash and backing away.

Another snowball flew past Wally and collided with Hunter's face.

"You little shits," Hunter cried, "I'm going to tell on you." He cradled his hand into his stomach. Blood soaked into his shirt and dripped onto the ground.

"You just said a bad word! We're telling on you," Sarah shouted back.

Hunter backed up the steps and toward the door. "I'm calling the police and telling them you stole our dog and attacked us. I'm bleeding."

"You hate Bop," Lenny protested. "Why can't they have him?"

"Because he's our dog! And I'm telling Mom on you when she gets home," Hunter said.

"I didn't do anything," Lenny said.

Another snowball whizzed past Wally and collided with Hunter's left ear.

"Stop it! Lenny, get the phone and call 911," Hunter commanded.

"But they're my friends," Lenny said.

Hunter backed inside the front door, shielding his face. "Do it," he declared.

Wally stood up next to Bop, who looked at him and wagged his tail. A red mark from the leash burned on his wrist and his stomach was coiled into a knot. "We'll come play your dungeon game if you let us have Bop," Wally pleaded to Hunter.

"Too late, Lenny come inside," Hunter said.

"Wally's dad is really sad and needs him," Sarah said.

Wally didn't want to have the police called on him. He knew his dad would be mad if he got in more trouble. Wally walked Bop to the front door and held his leash out to Hunter.

"Wally, don't do it!" Sarah shouted.

"Lenny, get the leash," Hunter commanded, taking a step back from Bop.

Lenny started crying as he took the leash from Wally. "I'm sorry," he said through a quiet sob.

"Please let us have him," Wally pleaded.

Hunter put his hand on the doorknob and paused, then he turned back toward Sarah and Wally, "I'll let you buy him for a thousand dollars."

"But I only have three dollars left," Sarah protested.

"Not my problem. Come back if you want to buy him," Hunter said. Lenny dipped his head down and let Hunter usher him back inside. The sound of Hunter slamming the door shut echoed off the snow-covered trees and cars.

Wally missed Bop and worried Hunter might hurt him. He realized now that maybe Sarah was right. Maybe Bop could make his dad happy.

Sarah turned around and marched away from Lenny's house. "I have an idea!" she yelled back at Wally. Wally ran to catch up.

CHAPTER 8

THE ELF MOM

SARAH OPENED the door to the basement and marched down the stairs.

Wally waited at the top of the steps and whispered, "Are you sure we shouldn't ask your dad?"

"My mom says he's cheap and never buys anything expensive," Sarah said. "Besides, he'll be too busy playing to notice."

Wally followed Sarah to the basement landing. Mr. Evans was wearing his cape and wizard hat and was leaning over a giant table. Two video cameras hung from the ceiling, one pointing straight down at the middle of the table and the other facing Mr. Evans. The room was dark except for a red light that pulsed over Mr. Evans's head. Creepy music overlayed with howling wind played through the speakers on the corners of the table.

Mr. Evans spoke in a high-pitched but soft voice like a girl, "How dare you break into my sacred dungeon. As queen of this realm, I hereby sentence you to a lifetime serving me. Take this!" Mr. Evans switched back to his normal voice, "Estrella is going to cast Gooify at third level, targeted at Bramble."

Sarah walked past Mr. Evans into a living room on the other side, where Eileen's eyes were glued to the TV. She sat on the ground in her diaper and with a pair of red headphones wrapped around the top of her head.

A die bounced to a halt on Mr. Evans's table. "That's a nat eighteen," he said.

Sarah swiped her dad's wallet off the coffee table next to the sofa. "See," she said, holding the wallet up to Wally's face.

Sarah opened the wallet and rummaged through the various pockets. "He doesn't have any money in here."

"Daddy!" Eileen called. She pointed at Wally and Sarah, but remained seated with her headphones on.

Sarah put her pointer finger up to her lips. "Shhh," she huffed at Eileen.

"Daddy. Daddy!"

Mr. Evans looked up and turned his head sideways when he noticed Sarah holding his wallet, "Guys, I'm gonna go on mute for a minute."

Wally's heart pounded in his chest. He didn't want to get in trouble again.

"Sarah, what are you doing?" Mr. Evans asked.

Eileen was facing the TV again and no longer paying attention.

"We need money to buy Bop from Lenny."

"Sarah, come on," Mr. Evans sighed. He walked over and held his hand out for the wallet, "It's almost Christmas, we're not buying anything. You'll just have to wait until Santa comes."

"But Wally's dad—"

"The answer is NO."

Sarah threw the wallet at the ground and ran toward the stairs. Wally followed her and heard Mr. Evans return to the game as he climbed the steps.

Later that night Wally sat at the dinner table with Sarah, Mr. Evans, and Eileen eating pot roast with carrots. Wally didn't normally like carrots, but he liked these because they were soft and tasted good. He wished he and his dad sat down to eat dinner like this.

"What'd you do at Lenny's house?" Mr. Evans asked Sarah and Wally.

"We played dolls," Sarah lied.

"With Lenny?" Mr. Evans said.

Sarah nodded her head, "It was his idea. Hunter played too."

Mr. Evans raised his eyebrow. "Huh," he said, shoving a bite of meat into his mouth.

Eileen reached her arm out and dropped a slice of carrot on the floor. "Oops!" she said giggling.

"Eileen, no playing with food," Mr. Evans told her.

When he leaned over to pick up the carrot, Eileen jumped onto the table, reached into Mr. Evans's bowl, and picked up a chunk of meat the size of a baseball.

"Eileen, what are you doing?" he shouted. He grabbed Eileen by the armpit and placed her back in her seat.

Eileen snickered as she ripped a chunk of flesh from the steak, "Yum!"

Wally leaned over and whispered to Sarah, "Do you think Bop's OK?"

"You don't?"

"Hunter's really mean. I think we need to rescue him."

"Don't worry," Sarah said, "my mom has all the money. She'll buy Bop for us."

After dinner, Wally and Sarah lounged in their fort. They hadn't yet turned on the string lights that ran in a grid overhead. The sun was setting outside, painting the snowy landscape baby blue and purple. Wally held *Mystery Ranch* in his hand, but it wasn't open.

"I hope my mom buys Bop," Sarah sighed.

"I don't think Bop can talk," Wally replied.

"Do you have any better ideas?"

"I think my dad wants a mom for me," Wally said.

"Why?" Sarah asked.

"Because he says he has two jobs since he has to take care of me. But your mom and dad each do one job."

"When did your mom die?"

"My dad said when I was a baby."

"Maybe Principal Anderson can be your mom. My dad thinks she's really pretty," Sarah said.

Wally shot up to a seat at the thought of that coming true. He liked Principal Anderson, but he didn't want to live with the principal. "Do you think my dad does?" Wally asked.

"Probably. My dad says when her ears stick through her hair she kinda looks like an elf from *Lord of the Rings* and that's his favorite movie."

Wally's dad liked *Lord of the Rings* too. It was the only PG-13 movie he'd been allowed to watch. When Wally and Sarah were younger, Wally's dad used to dress up like a dwarf and play games with Mr. Evans.

"Your dad doesn't want a mom, though," Sarah told Wally.

Wally tilted his head, "How do you know?"

"I heard my mom say that your dad's met all her friends and he still doesn't like any of them. She was really mad."

"When did he meet them?"

Sarah shrugged her shoulders, "I think when Lenny's brother babysits us they take your dad to meet moms."

Wally had never thought about if his dad had already looked for a mom. "You don't think that's the meaning of life?" he replied.

"No, my dad told my mom he likes being alone."

Wally tossed the book on the ground and pushed his palms into his eyes. All of their leads had dried up. Tomorrow was Christmas Eve and they still had no idea where to find the meaning of life. He wanted to cry and scream at the same time, but only tears came out. "I don't want my dad to be sad anymore," he weeped.

Sarah wrapped her arm around Wally, "I checked Alexa and her idea is coming tomorrow."

Wally lowered his hands from his face. He'd forgotten about Alexa. "When?" he asked.

"In the morning."

Wally remained silent.

"I still think Bop knows," Sarah said.

CHAPTER 9

THE DRAGON TOY

WHEN WALLY and Sarah woke up on Christmas Eve, the sun was shining through the window making it difficult to see. The air outside was still and looked slightly foggy in the morning light.

A large stack of waffles was waiting for Wally and Sarah on the kitchen table when they ventured downstairs for breakfast. The smell of bacon engulfed the room and made Wally's stomach growl, but Eileen had the plate of bacon on her lap and looked as possessive of it as Bee Bee had about the rib bone a few days earlier. He didn't ask for any.

Wally and Sarah each covered a large waffle in maple syrup, then skewered it with their forks and ate it bite by bite. Syrup dripped onto the table and floor, which Bee Bee was quick to clean up.

"Alright you four," Mr. Evans said. He held a coffee mug in his left hand that had a picture of a wizard and a die with the number twenty on it. He was still wearing his sweats and cape, only today he had on a red Santa hat instead of the wizard hat. "I need you all to behave for a few hours. Daddy has his DnD stream again."

"But you just did that," Sarah complained.

"We have to do a Christmas Eve special, but then I won't do it for a few weeks if that makes you feel better."

"But isn't it make believe?"

"Yes, but it's like a make-believe video game."

"Then why do you need Christmas in make believe?"

"Because the characters we're pretending to be still like Christmas."

"But they don't need presents. They can have anything they want."

"Christmas isn't just about presents."

Sarah scowled at her dad while taking a bite of syrup-saturated waffle.

"Eileen, you're coming down with me today," Mr. Evans said, picking her up from the chair. She was still wearing only a diaper and she took the plate of bacon with her.

Wally and Sarah checked the delivery status of *The Meaning of Life* three times, but Alexa kept telling them the item was "out for delivery."

Later that morning, Mr. Evans laughed in the basement so loudly Wally and Sarah could hear him while they were half-heartedly playing detective upstairs in Sarah's room.

When the doorbell rang, Wally took off running down the stairs. Sarah followed. They peered through the narrow glass window beside the front door. Wally's heart raced when he saw a large cardboard box sealed with green tape covered in pine trees and the Amazon Prime logo.

"That's it!" Sarah exclaimed.

She reached her hand up to open the door, but Wally interrupted her, "We're not supposed to answer the door alone."

"We're not kids anymore, Wally," Sarah chided him.

Sarah unlocked the door and swung it open. A man with long dreadlocks was jogging toward an idling blue van on the street. Sarah squatted and extended her arms all the way out on both sides, bear hugging the package. Wally tiptoed around Sarah and grabbed the box from the other side. Together they managed to pick it up and shuffle through the doorway, but dropped it to the ground as soon as they were inside far enough to close the door.

Wally ferociously ripped the tape off, throwing strips onto the ground behind him with each swipe, then bent the cardboard lids open. The first item was in a long box that had a picture of a blue dragon toy on it.

"Bad Dr...Dra..." Wally said, sounding out the words on the box.

"Dragon!" Sarah shouted, reading over his shoulder.

Wally pulled the top of the box off.

"This is for Bee Bee. My dad threw her other dragon toy away," Sarah explained.

Wally plunged his hand into the box and pulled out a large piece of blue rubber. It was long and had lots of edges on it that made it look like a dragon head. The toy bobbled back and forth in his hand as he waved it in the air.

"What is it?" Wally asked.

"A dragon!" Sarah replied. "...Or maybe a bone?"

The sound of Bee Bee's nails scraping against the floor as she rose from her nap and barreled toward them echoed from the mud room. When her large head came into view, Wally became acutely aware that he was holding Bee Bee's new toy. He turned his head and saw Bee Bee trotting toward them wagging her tail.

Wally's first instinct was to get rid of the toy, but then he remembered how nice Bop had been. He took a deep breath and clutched the dragon with both hands. Bee Bee skidded to a stop just in front of him and sat expectantly.

"You can throw it," Sarah told Wally.

Wally wound his arm up and chucked the toy over Bee Bee's head. "Fetch!" he yelled. The toy landed on the floor, bounced three times, then rolled to a stop under the couch in the living room. Bee Bee took off, slipping on the rug in the entryway.

Excitement built in Wally's chest, the meaning of life felt close. Next, he pulled a plastic-wrapped set of paper towels from the box. "Those are for my dad," Sarah said.

Wally dropped the paper towels, bent down, and rummaged through crumpled brown paper stuffed inside the box. "This must be it," he said, lifting a small book from the box with both hands.

Sarah scrunched her eyebrows. "It's a book?"

Wally opened the book to the first page and read, "Dear thee. Thee?... Dear thee read—er. This is your first step twor... twor-ard cra...craf...craft-ing your new life. Your new life of me...meee...meaning. My name is Dr. John Ritcher, and I'm going to teach you how to live—" Wally looked up at Sarah, "I don't think this is it."

"Why?" Sarah asked.

"My dad's read every book. Even your dad said that was true."

Sarah grabbed the book and flipped through a few more pages, "You're right, he's probably read this." She dropped it back into the box.

Wally felt the muscles around his mouth sag with disappointment. They were out of time and out of ideas. If his dad, Mr. Evans, and Alexa couldn't find the meaning of life, it didn't seem like anybody could. Bop was their last hope. "Do you really think Bop knows?" he asked Sarah.

Sarah nodded her head.

Across the room, Bee Bee rammed the corner of the couch with her shoulder. The couch legs moaned as they slid across the hardwood floor, colliding with a tall black lamp on the other side. The lamp wobbled, then fell forward onto a glass coffee table. The metal lampshade bounced on impact, causing the glass to shatter and fall into the fibers of a white rug that had fur as long as Bee Bee's.

Wally heard Mr. Evans running up the stairs before he saw him. "What happened?!" Mr. Evans shouted.

Wally and Sarah stood near the box, unsure if they'd done something wrong or if just Bee Bee would be in trouble. Mr. Evans looked at them, cocking his head slightly. Then Bee Bee walked proudly from the living room to Mr. Evans, shaking the blue dragon back and forth before dropping it at his feet.

"What...? Sarah, did you give that to her? How did...

Where... What are you doing?" he stammered, broadening his arms away from his body.

"We were throwing Bee Bee's new dragon," she replied.

"Sarah, I'm in the middle of my stream. Go to your room now."

Mr. Evans bent down, snatched the slobbery toy off the ground, and wrapped it inside of his cloak. He briefly hovered over the rug, inspecting the broken glass, then grabbed Bee Bee's collar and escorted her to the basement door. "Sarah, now!" Mr. Evans shouted, pointing toward the staircase.

"Let's go to the fort," Sarah said to Wally. "I have an idea."

Wally and Sarah scurried across the room and up the stairs.

"And stay off the rug!" Mr. Evans shouted just before he slammed the basement door shut.

CHAPTER 10

THE WRECKING BALL

WALLY STACKED a red Lego piece onto the castle he and Sarah were building in the living room. Mr. Evans had rolled up the rug and dragged it outside along with the broken table after his stream, creating an open space to play on. Sarah told Wally her mom liked it when she played with Legos because they were her favorite toy when she was a kid, so if they had them out when she got home, she'd be extra nice.

Wally was skeptical. "But how many ice cream cones is a thousand dollars?" he asked.

"I think about a thousand," Sarah replied.

"Your mom will give us that much?"

"Whenever my mom comes back from trips she takes us shopping and buys us lots of stuff."

Mr. Evans told them that Mrs. Evans would return shortly after breakfast, but they had finished eating a long time ago and she still wasn't home.

A chorus of icicles breaking off the house and snowmelt running through the gutters filled an otherwise quiet house as the morning crept into afternoon. All of their Lego pieces were used to construct a multi-colored castle, complete with city walls that spanned the floorspace of the living room. The twinkling lights from the Christmas tree in the corner of the room brightened their diorama with red and green tints. Sarah was sure her mom would be impressed.

They lay on the floor next to their creation while they waited for Mrs. Evans. Sarah broke the silence, "My daddy said your dad is sick."

"I think he's just sad," Wally explained. "He said he'd be OK soon."

"My dad said the doctors are giving him a potion that will make him better."

Wally's dad hadn't told him about a potion. He stared at the ceiling, wondering if what Sarah said was true.

Sarah interrupted Wally's thought. "My mom's home!" she exclaimed, pointing out the window.

A black Tesla rolled down the street toward the Evanses' house. Mr. Norris was outside again and tried to stop Mrs. Evans, but she swerved around him without slowing down and pulled into the driveway.

"OK, just remember, if my mom says no the first time, you have to cry. Sometimes it works. I'll handle the rest," Sarah said.

Wally wasn't sure he knew how to fake crying, but he followed Sarah to the garage door and waited for Mrs. Evans to come in. Mr. Evans emerged from the basement with Eileen and Bee Bee as the sound of the garage door closing rumbled the walls of the house.

When Mrs. Evans cracked the garage door open both Sarah and Eileen called out, "Mommy, Mommy, Mommy!"

Sarah narrowed her eyebrows at her dad when he stepped in front of her. "How was your trip, Sweetie?" Mr. Evans asked.

Mrs. Evans looked a lot like Sarah, just more grown up—she was tall and slender and had long black hair. Her belly protruded from her body, stretching her beige knitted sweater. Sarah told Wally she hoped she'd get a little brother, but her parents had told her the doctor looked inside her belly and saw it was a girl.

"I just got off the phone with Mark. Sandra is still being a stick in the mud with the whole Rooney contract," Mrs. Evans complained. "And this random guy on the plane came over to me and told me I shouldn't be flying this pregnant. People need to mind their own business."

Sarah shuffled around Mr. Evans to get back into Mrs. Evans's view. "Mommy!" she tried again.

Mrs. Evans pulled Sarah onto her leg and hugged her with one arm, "I've missed you, Sarah. How was your last week of school?"

"Mrs. Brenda kept calling it Christmas break and I corrected her that it was holiday break like you said because not everyone celebrates Christmas," Sarah rambled.

"Good job, I'm proud of you for standing up for yourself," Mrs. Evans replied.

Eileen rested on Mr. Evans's hip in her diaper. "Daddy says Santa's bringing me presents," she said.

Mrs. Evans leaned down and kissed Eileen's forehead, "That will be so exciting."

"Mommy!" Sarah yelled.

"Yes, Sarah?"

Sarah pulled on her mother's pants, "Mommy, Wally and I made a huge Lego castle. Come see."

"I can get your bags from the car," Mr. Evans said.

"Thanks, Sam." Mrs. Evans leaned over and kissed Mr. Evans on the lips.

When she turned around, she picked up a can off the counter that had snowmen on it and said "Snow in a Can." "Sam, what's this? I've told you before this stuff is full of neurotoxins and is very dangerous. I don't want it around the kids."

"It was on sale and said it's 'natural,'" Mr. Evans explained. "I thought it might be OK?"

Mrs. Evans set the can back on the counter, shaking her head.

"Mommy, Sarah said a bad word," Eileen shouted at Mrs. Evans.

"No I didn't!" Sarah contested.

"Nobody did anything bad," Mr. Evans said. "We've all been good and are glad Mommy's home."

Eileen shook her head, "In the car, Sarah said a bad word."

Sarah pointed her finger at Eileen. "That was you," she shot back. Her face was turning red.

"No it wasn't," Eileen whined. She started crying, "Ahhh!"

Mr. Evans slipped through the garage door, leaving Mrs. Evans with Sarah and Wally. Eileen's sobs echoed in the garage as Sarah grabbed her mom's hand and dragged her toward their Lego castle.

"Look what we made," Sarah said. She pointed her big eyes up at her mom, who lowered down to her knees and inspected their work.

"Wow, very good," Mrs. Evans said.

"Is it better than the best one you've ever made?" Sarah asked.

"I made some pretty good ones, but I think this is the best."

Sarah approached her mom and looked her in the eyes. Her mom reached her hands out and grabbed Sarah's. "Mommy?" Sarah asked.

"Yes?"

"Can Wally and I have one thousand dollars?"

Mrs. Evans turned her head sideways, "What do you need that much money for?"

"Because Wally's dad is really sad and he got in trouble at school for trying to figure out why so now we need to buy Lenny's dog Bop, but Hunter will only let us have him for one thousand dollars because we left the door open and Bop got out but Wally bonked his head and Bop saved him and—" Sarah rambled.

"Woah, slow down, Sarah," Mrs. Evans said. "Lenny's brother...Hunter?" she clarified. Sarah nodded her head and Mrs. Evans continued, "...Wants you to pay him one thousand dollars to buy their dog?"

"Please," Sarah begged.

"We already have Bee Bee."

"No, we need Bop for Wally," Sarah clarified.

"I don't think Wally's dad has time to take care of a dog right now."

Wally spoke up, "We think Bop would make him happy."

Wally felt tears building in his eyes. He didn't have to pretend to cry. Mrs. Evans looked at him and for a brief moment the house was so silent, Wally could hear snow melting off the roof again.

Mr. Evans swung the garage door open and stumbled inside. He had a duffle bag and purse slung over each shoulder, a large Starbucks coffee in one hand, and a rolling suitcase in the other. Eileen squeezed between him and the door jam, then ran toward them. "Ahhhhh!" she cried.

Eileen held her sippy cup by the handle and sprinted across the room in her diaper. Her mouth was opened wide as she screamed, exposing her pointing canines. At first, it looked like she was going to run into Mrs. Evans's open arms, but at the last moment she diverted her path around Mrs. Evans. "I came in like a wrecking ball!" she yelled, swinging her sippy cup into the wall of Sarah and Wally's castle.

Bam!

Red and green Lego pieces sprayed in all directions, some hitting the window across the room. Eileen wound back up and swung again.

Bang!

This time the drawbridge and entrance crumbled under the blow of the sippy cup.

Sarah sprang to her feet. "Eileen!" she yelled.

Eileen paused and looked at Sarah with her brows narrowed and venom in her eyes. Her mouth bent up into a sadistic grin, then she grabbed her sippy cup with both hands, wound up with her entire torso, and swung it into the castle's tallest tower.

Boom!

Lego pieces exploded off the bottom of the sippy cup as the tower toppled to the ground, smashing into the horse stables and swimming pool Wally and Sarah had built.

Mrs. Evans lost her balance as she reached for Eileen and rolled onto her side.

"Amy!" Mr. Evans called, throwing the suitcase to the ground. He was still tethered to her bags as he ran toward her and tripped on one of Bee Bee's toys, stumbling into a face plant. His cheek made a screeching sound against the hardwood floor as the bags tumbled on top of him. "Are you OK?" he grunted from a few paces away. He started shedding the bags on his shoulders.

Bam! Bam! Bang!

Eileen Hulk-smashed smaller buildings in the castle's city walls as fast as she could. "Ehehe! Ehe!" she laughed.

Mrs. Evans rolled onto her side, "I think—" she started to say, but she was interrupted by Sarah's war cry as she charged across the room toward Eileen.

"Grrraah!" Sarah grunted, ramming her shoulder into Eileen's chest. Her impact launched both of the sisters into the air. Eileen's back made a solid thud as they smashed into the ground. Sarah grabbed her little sister's right arm and forced her onto her stomach as she shouted, "Hands behind your back, criminal."

"Sarah, let go right now," Mr. Evans commanded. He sounded really mad and was running at them.

"She wrecked our castle," Sarah shouted back.

Eileen's nose and stomach were squished against the floor as her legs flailed in the air. "Ahhhaa!" she sobbed. "Daddy!"

Mrs. Evans slowly pushed herself up to a seat. "Sarah, let Eileen go," she calmly commanded.

Sarah hopped off her sister and bent over the demolished Lego castle to inspect the damage. Wally took a step backward, unsure of who would be in trouble. Maybe all of them?

Eileen stood up and ran into Mr. Evans's arms. "Sarah and Eileen," Mr. Evans reprimanded them as he picked up Eileen.

"Aha!...Ahhh!...Ahhhh!" Eileen cried out. Her face was red and she kicked her feet back and forth in Mr. Evans's cradle.

"Sam, I've got Sarah. Take Eileen up for her nap," Mrs. Evans said.

"I don't need a nap," Eileen yelled. "I! Don't! Need! NAP!"

Mr. Evans doubled over briefly when one of Eileen's thrashing legs kicked him in the stomach. He turned her around and held her at arm's length as he ascended the stairs.

"STOP!" she yelled. "NO!"

When Eileen's bedroom door upstairs shut, Mrs. Evans took a deep breath, then addressed Sarah and Wally, "I'm sorry about your castle. I know you worked hard on it."

Eileen's cries continued to echo throughout the house and were rising to a higher pitch, "No!...NOOO!"

Sarah and Wally both had real tears in their eyes. They looked to Mrs. Evans, waiting for her to continue talking. She closed her eyes briefly and rubbed her temples.

"I'll tell you what," Mrs. Evans said as she pushed herself to her feet, "I'm going to give you one hundred dollars as an early

Christmas present. How about during holiday break, you and Wally think of a business you can start with a hundred dollars that will make one thousand. I can help you."

"But Wally wants to give his dad Bop for Christmas tomorrow!" Sarah argued.

Mrs. Evans waddled to her black purse on the ground and squatted to pick it up. "Well, we're going to have to talk with Wally's dad first before we send him home with a dog anyway. We can ask tomorrow when he comes over." She opened up her wallet and slid a crisp one-hundred-dollar bill out. "For now, how about you focus on this project." She handed Wally the money.

Wally had only held a fifty-dollar bill once and never a one-hundred-dollar bill. He didn't know what to do with it.

"Maybe you two can buy shovels and help everyone shovel their driveways," Mrs. Evans suggested. She grabbed her suitcase and sauntered toward the staircase.

Wally turned to face Sarah, "Now what?"

Sarah shrugged her shoulders, "I wish we brought our eraser shavings home. We could sell them."

Wally nodded his head, "I think I have an idea."

CHAPTER 11

THE CHOCOLATE FIRE STAND

"ARE you sure this is gonna work?" Sarah asked.

"No," Wally admitted, "but one time my dad bought some from a kid."

Wally stepped onto a chair and pulled a pitcher of boiling water out of the microwave.

Sarah taped four pieces of green construction paper together and picked up a gold marker. "What should we call it?" Sarah asked.

"Christmas drink?" Wally suggested.

Sarah's eyes widened, "How about chocolate fire?"

"Why fire?" Wally asked.

"We can put it in the microwave for a long time and make it hot like fire to keep people warm, since it's cold out," Sarah explained.

Wally nodded his head, "OK, should I put it in longer?"

"Ya," Sarah said. "And put some tinfoil over the top. My dad does that when he wants to keep things warm."

Wally pulled a roll of tinfoil from a drawer near the microwave and tore off a sheet. "Where's the hot chocolate packs?" Wally asked.

Sarah pointed to the pantry, "Next to the animal crackers."

Wally dragged the chair into the pantry and searched for the packets of hot chocolate Mr. Evans made for them some days after school, but he couldn't find any. "I can't find them," he hollered to Sarah.

Sarah ran into the pantry and checked behind every box and bag. "Eileen must have drank all of them," she complained.

Wally picked up a Snickers bar, "What about these?"

"Do they melt?" Sarah asked.

Wally opened the wrapper and hustled over to the pitcher of hot water. He dropped the Snickers bar in. The chocolate coating of the bar melted into the water, staining it a tinge of brown.

"Get more," Sarah said.

Wally ran back into the pantry. "How many?"

"All of them!"

Wally opened ten Snickers bars and dropped them into the pitcher, one by one. Each bar dyed the water a darker shade of brown. By the time he was done, the liquid looked like hot chocolate.

Sarah drew flames onto the green sign using a red marker. "Done," Wally hollered over to her.

"Now add the fire!" Sarah said.

Wally put the sheet of tinfoil over the top of the pitcher and shoved it into the microwave. "How many minutes?"

"Five," Sarah said.

Wally started the microwave and lowered his head to look inside.

Pop! Pop!

To his surprise, real flames were burning on top of the drink.

"Fire!" Wally shouted.

"I told you, real fire!"

Sarah and Wally stepped back and watched the drink burst into bright flashes of light. Soon the fire went out and the pitcher spun in the microwave for several more minutes, the Snickers bars disintegrating in the boiling water.

When the timer went off, Wally pulled the pitcher from the microwave. A burnt smell rushed out of the enclosure that made Wally feel a little dizzy. He noticed black marks on the ceiling of the microwave where the flames had hit and hoped Mr. Evans wouldn't be mad.

Sarah marched toward the garage door carrying the green sign in both hands, "Let's go."

The sun wasn't setting yet, but it had dipped below the crest of the mountains. Wally still didn't have gloves, so he held onto the pitcher of hot chocolate for warmth. Bits of nuts and brown foam floated at the top. A green sign flapped in a crisp breeze from the edge of their folding table. Red flames encircled golden letters on the sign that read:

ChoЖolat Fire
$1000

Mr. Norris was rearranging his reindeer again and sauntered over when he finished.

"What are you selling?" he asked.

"Chocolate Fire," Sarah said.

"One thousand dollars!" Mr. Norris cried. "Is this in Chinese dollars or Monopoly money?"

"No," Wally replied. "We need it to buy a dog."

Mr. Norris bent down and inspected the pitcher in the evening's dimming twilight. "What's all that crap floating in there?"

"That's from the fire," Wally explained.

"Don't tell him the secret recipe," Sarah said.

Mr. Norris pulled a leather wallet from his back pocket that was overflowing with receipts. "I'll give you a buck for a cup."

"No," Sarah declared.

He pulled out a dollar bill and extended it toward Wally. "Back when I was a kid, I'd be lucky to get a quarter at my lemonade stand. It's a good deal, kid."

A man with a white beard and long hair not unlike Mr. Norris hobbled up to the stand, "I could smell the chocolate."

"Get out of here, Pendle. Don't make me call the cops again."

Pendle had on five layers of visible jackets in all different colors. Mrs. Evans had told Sarah and Wally to come inside if Pendle ever approached them and that he smelled terrible. Wally thought he smelled a little bit like the boys' locker room at school, but it wasn't as bad as Mrs. Evans had told them.

Pendle crouched down and swung his arms back and forth like an ape, "I already called 'em, Geezer! Told 'em all about the prisoners you're torturing in your yard."

"For Christ's sake. Those are decorations." Mr. Norris turned and pointed his finger at Pendle, "Are you the one who's been moving them?"

Pendle tilted his head back and looked up at the sky. "Oh no, not me. I've been far far away in a galaxy where everything's pink," Pendle declared. He held up a tattered leather leash, "Lost my dog on the comet ride home. He wanted to visit his friends on the moon for a while."

Wally and Sarah met each other's gaze. Wally grabbed the pitcher of Chocolate Fire and they both began backing their way slowly up the driveway.

"Hey! I need chocolate or I'll die. I need something to balance out the pink or I'll be sick something real serious," Pendle exclaimed.

"It's one thousand dollars," Sarah shouted from the middle of the driveway down to where Pendle and Mr. Norris were standing at the edge of the sidewalk.

"Deal," Pendle said. He pulled his fingers to his teeth and jumped up and down squealing with excitement, "Eeeh! Eeeh! Chocolate!"

"For Pete's sake, you don't have a thousand dollars," Mr. Norris cried.

Pendle widened his arms and spun in circles like a top, "I have a thousand dollars a millions times over..." He stopped and pointed at Mr. Norris, "but I hide my treasure chest in the Big Dipper so you don't steal it!"

"I've never stolen a thing in my life, you vagrant."

Pendle broke into an Irish river dance, moving his arms up and down as his feet tapped forward and back. "Sticks and stones may break my bones, but words will never hurt me." He finished with his arms out, jazzing his hands. Mrs. Evans had made Pendle seem scary, but Wally thought he was funny. He smiled and laughed at Pendle's bit.

"This is ridiculous." Mr. Norris reopened his wallet, "Here's ten dollars, it's more than you'll ever get out of this nutcase." He extended the money toward Wally.

Wally began to lift his hand up to the bill, but Pendle interrupted him, "I wouldn't go doing that now, young one. For while I do have all the money in the world I could offer you, I will trade you something much more valuable."

"I'm sick of this shit," Mr. Norris said. "Take the ten bucks or I'm leaving. I'm not gonna stand here and be ridiculed anymore."

Pendle spun his right pointer finger in circles near his temple and mouthed, "Crazy," as he pointed at Mr. Norris behind his back.

Wally hesitated. "What do you have?" he asked Pendle.

"Pshh!" Mr. Norris turned the other way and stomped across the street toward his house. "A million bucks my ass," he muttered to himself.

Pendle turned to Wally and bowed. "I see that you are wise

beyond your years. I should never have doubted you. There are many auras around your head. Many indeed."

Wally didn't know what to do, so he bowed back.

"And as a reward for your cunning and bravery, I'm willing to exchange this, my dog's magical leash and collar, for your pitcher of chocolate fire." He held out a brown leather leash connected to a matching collar. They were both covered in gashes and mud.

"We're getting a dog," Sarah exclaimed.

"I had a feeling," Pendle replied. He chuckled as he spoke, "Stardust can reveal many things."

"But where's your dog?" Wally asked. "The magical one?"

"Oh, on the comet ride back home he decided to stop over and visit friends on the moon. I'm not one to crash a party, so I tied a birthday hat on his head and sent him on his way."

Wally couldn't believe it. Was any of it true? "What does the leash do?" he asked.

Sarah shuffled over to Wally when Pendle bent down to whisper in Wally's ear. Pendle's breath smelled like trash, but Wally didn't mind. If Pendle's dog really was magic, maybe it was true that Bop was magic, too.

"What I'm about to tell you is ancient knowledge. Older than me or you or the trees themselves. To possess magic is both a blessing and a curse. Magic can be unwieldy and difficult to tame. Some souls are driven mad by its power. This collar and leash gives protection to whoever wears it against the negative effects of magic."

"What kind of magic does your dog know?" Sarah asked.

"Dogs possess more magic than we can ever learn or see!"

Pendle shouted. "But the most important thing he taught me was how to fly through space. I can't imagine ever being earthbound again."

"Your dog knows how to fly through space?" Wally clarified.

Pendle crossed his arms and stared at Wally, "He knows everything, but that is one among them."

"Does he know where to find the meaning of life?" Wally asked.

"Oh yes, he's showed me many times."

Sarah nudged Wally with her elbow, "I told you."

"Deal," Wally said. He reached his hand out to take the magic leash.

Sarah shot her arm in between Wally and Pendle, "What about the thousand dollars?"

"We can make it another way. We'll need this leash for Bop," Wally stated.

Sarah opened her mouth to say something, but no words came out. She relaxed her shoulder and replied, "You're right. We could never buy this."

Pendle handed Wally the leash and collar, then his hands sprang instantly to the pitcher of chocolate fire. He smiled and laughed as he brought the pitcher up to his mouth with both hands, "Tonight, I will harness the spirit of the dragon and breathe fire!" Pendle tipped the pitcher back and began chugging the liquid. After he drank about a fourth of it, he closed his eyes and slowly lowered the pitcher back down. "Ahhhhh..."

"Can you feel the fire?" Sarah asked.

Pendle made a sizzling sound with his tongue, then opened

his mouth suddenly and exhaled toward the sky. "Rrraaahh!" he wheezed, as if fire was also coming out of his mouth.

"Oh yes, this is the best chocolate fire I've ever had," Pendle declared. "And now, I bid you adieu." Pendle turned and sprinted toward the trail at the end of the street with the pitcher before banking right into the trees where he lived.

Headlights on a black SUV appeared in the distance and sped toward Wally and Sarah.

"I like him," Sarah said, "he's funny."

Wally agreed. "And he's even had chocolate fire before."

The SUV slowed near the driveway, sliding a few feet as it came to a stop. The window rolled down and Lenny stuck his head out. Hunter was in the seat next to him with a pair of headphones anchored to his head.

Wally ran to the car and jumped onto the running board to get his face level with Lenny's. "Is Bop with you?" he asked.

Jason, Hunter and Lenny's sixteen-year-old brother, was driving. He slouched in the front seat with the hood of his black jacket up. The last time Jason babysat Wally, Sarah, and Lenny, he drove them to a sandwich shop by the college that smelled like skunks. Jason glanced at Wally and waved, then shifted his attention back to his phone.

"No," Lenny sniffled, "we just dropped him off at the Humane Society." A tear rolled down Lenny's face, which he rubbed off with the back of his hand.

"Why did you do that?" Wally asked.

"He pooped on Hunter's pillow," Lenny replied, "and ate butt holes in all my mom's underwear."

"I thought you were going to give him to us?" Sarah asked.

"My mom wouldn't let me. She said she wanted him out or Santa wouldn't come."

Jason threw his phone onto the dashboard shelf and turned the stereo volume up. "Time to wrap it up, Lenny boy. I just got a ride," he hollered back at them.

"I'll come over and show you my presents tomorrow if I'm not grounded," Lenny said, wiping another tear from his face, "Merry Christmas."

Jason started rolling the window up, so Sarah and Wally jumped down. The car sped off down the street, drifting in the snow around the corner.

"Fuckin' kids, slow down!" Mr. Norris yelled from his yard.

Wally looked at Sarah, "We have to rescue Bop," he said.

CHAPTER 12

THE SCHEME

WALLY AND SARAH huddled in their blanket fort, organizing the items they'd collected from around the house.

"You don't have to come with me," Wally said. He fastened the Velcro of a Spider-Man silly string shooter onto his right wrist. "We'll probably get in trouble."

"We have to rescue Bop and help your dad," Sarah replied. "Don't worry, I'm good at getting out of trouble. All I have to do is cry and say I missed my mom while she was gone and she always gets me out of trouble." She shoved a can with a snowman on it into her purple unicorn backpack.

"What's that stuff do?" Wally asked.

"My mom said it shoots out toxic snow and is very dangerous," Sarah told him.

Wally slid a small hammer with a pointed face into the backpack. "I saw bigger hammers in the garage," he told Sarah.

"This one's magic. My mom says if the car ever crashes into a lake, we could use this to break all the windows."

"When can we get his phone?" Wally asked.

Sarah pressed her ear up against the wall between her room and Eileen's room. "I think they're almost done. My dad always goes downstairs to play *Call of Duty* after he puts Eileen to bed."

Wally slid both of his suction cup arrows into his quiver, checking to make sure they were still straight by looking down the shaft with one eye.

When Bee Bee scratched at the door, Wally tiptoed over and opened the door to let her in. She was carrying the rubber dragon toy again.

"Where did you get that?" Sarah sighed.

Bee Bee dropped the toy on Sarah's lap and wagged her tail.

"We should bring it," Wally said, "for Bop."

"Good idea," Sarah replied. She stuffed it into her backpack.

Wally and Sarah looked at each other when they heard the faint creak of Mr. Evans closing Eileen's bedroom door. They sat in silence for several minutes, waiting to make sure Mr. Evans had time to go downstairs. At one point they thought they heard someone walking down the hallway, but when Sarah checked, she didn't see anyone.

When the daylight finally faded completely into night, Wally wrapped the dog leash and collar around his torso like a sash, then slung his bow and quiver around his right shoulder. "Ready?" he asked, pulling a black ski mask over his face.

Sarah did the same, then zipped up her backpack and secured it on her shoulders, "Let's rescue Bop."

As Sarah peered through her cracked bedroom door, the sound of a door shutting downstairs echoed throughout the house. "I think he just went downstairs," Sarah said.

Wally and Sarah crawled on the floor out of Sarah's room and down the staircase. The house was dark and quiet until they reached the bottom of the stairs, when they noticed light shining from the inside of the refrigerator. The door was opened toward them, blocking their view of who was concealed behind it. Sarah scurried across the room and hid behind the corner of a wall, but tripped on her way and fell onto her hands and knees.

The refrigerator door slowly closed, revealing the hidden person. Eileen was standing in the dim light of the refrigerator in her pajamas with a giant plastic jug of eggnog clutched in both hands. The chest of her pink pajamas was drenched and the syrupy drink dripped from her chin and nose into a puddle on the ground. She tipped the jug into the air over her head and chugged the drink.

A buzzing sound rang from the direction of the kitchen counter. Sarah hustled and snatched it, then held her dad's phone toward Wally. "Now we don't have to go downstairs," Sarah said. "Let's get out of here."

Eileen tilted the container of eggnog up in the air, dumping the remaining liquid onto her face. She threw the empty container on the ground, then reopened the refrigerator. It sounded like she was climbing onto one of the shelves. Wally and Sarah took the opportunity to sneak through the back door and gingerly opened the fence gate. As they crawled below the bushes along the property line between the Evanses and their neighbors, Wally noticed Mr. and Mrs. Evans across the street.

Wally tapped Sarah on the shoulder and pointed. "Look," he whispered.

Mrs. Evans was moving Mr. Norris's reindeer on top of each other like they were when they got home from school and Mr. Norris was mad. Mr. Evans was doubled over laughing, then dragged Santa behind one of the deer and put another deer behind Santa resting its legs on his shoulders.

"What are they doing?" Wally whispered.

Sarah shrugged her shoulders, "My mom hates Mr. Norris."

Wally and Sarah crawled down the sidewalk, using trees and bushes for cover. When they turned the corner and were out of sight of Mr. and Mrs. Evans, Sarah pulled her dad's phone out. "Siri, I need an Uber," she said.

Siri responded, "What type of ride do you want? UberX... Select...Comfort—"

"UberX," Sarah replied.

"Uber can get you a ride in two minutes. Would you like me to request it?"

"Yes."

"OK, your Uber ride with Richard is on its way. He'll be driving a black Escalade with license plate 'STU-FIT.'"

A few seconds later a black SUV sped past Sarah and Wally. It turned around at the end of the street, then zoomed back in their direction. Mr. Evans's phone rang and Sarah answered.

"Did you order an Uber? I'm outside," a young male voice responded.

"We're right here," Sarah said. "Slow down!"

Sarah ran to the curb and waved the SUV down. When it came to a park, Wally heard the doors unlock and opened the door to the back seat.

"Hey, what are you guys doing?" the guy in the front seat asked.

"Wait, your name's Jason, not Richard," Sarah said.

Jason spun around in his seat, "I had to use my dad's license to start the Uber account."

"We're going to rescue Bop," Sarah explained, climbing into the car. Wally followed and slammed the door shut.

"My dog, Bop?" Jason asked.

"Ya, we want to take him home to help my dad," Wally said.

Jason moaned, "My parents just made us drop him off at the Humane Society."

"We asked Hunter if we could have him and he told us we had to pay a thousand dollars," Sarah complained.

"Hunter's a prick. He's the reason we had to get rid of Bop. He was supposed to be my dog."

"I think Hunter is really mean," Sarah agreed.

Jason smiled, "Lenny told me you guys made him cry?"

"We did," Sarah said. "If you take us to the Humane Society, next time you watch us I'll make him cry again."

Jason laughed, then took a deep breath and pressed a few buttons on the phone mounted to the dashboard. "I should really take you both home," he said.

"But we need to rescue Bop," Wally pleaded. "He can't spend Christmas at the pound."

"They closed right as we left," Jason said. "I don't think anyone will be there."

"We're breaking him out," Wally explained.

"You could help us?" Sarah suggested.

"Oh no. If you guys break the law, it's cute. If I do it, I'll go to jail."

Jason bit his lip and stared into the night. "You'll use that phone to call your parents for help if you need it? You're not going to get hurt or die or something?"

Sarah nodded her head, "My dad's a really fast driver."

Jason pulled the hood of his jacket over his head like he'd had it earlier in the day and sat for a moment in silence. Small snowflakes fell onto the windshield, melting on impact. He spun back around to face them. "I tell you what. Bop is a good boy and my parents will never let us take him back. I'll drop you there, but you have to swear you never saw me or got in the car."

"Deal," Wally said.

"Deal," Sarah agreed.

"And that if there's anything dangerous, you'll call your parents right away. Don't call me. Understand?"

Wally and Sarah nodded their heads.

Jason turned his phone off, slid it into his pocket, then put the car in drive. He whipped the front end around, running over the curb with one of the tires, then turned up the radio. A choir sang "Silent Night" as they drifted around an icy corner at the bottom of the street.

CHAPTER 13

THE JAILBREAK

JASON SLOWED the car and turned his headlights off when they turned onto the Humane Society's street. "I'm going to drive behind the building, stop briefly for you to get out, then circle back. OK?"

Wally nocked an arrow on his bow. "OK," he whispered.

As the car creeped past the back entrance of the building, Wally hopped to the ground and did a somersault into the grass on the other side of the sidewalk. Sarah followed and pushed the door shut. They ran into the bushes as Jason coasted down the street and turned out of sight.

Sarah pointed at the building and set her backpack in the grass. "That's the door where the dogs are," she said, pulling the small, pointed hammer out of her backpack.

Wally readied his bow and ran, crouching along the edge of the building. He peered through the glass door and investigated the dark room. One of the dogs started barking, then two more joined in and he could see blurry shapes moving in the darkness.

"Coast is clear," Wally whispered. The breeze rushing onto his body was frigid, but his hands were sweating.

Sarah ran at the entrance and swung the hammer from above her head like an axe, striking the center of the glass door. The glass shattered on impact, thousands of little pieces falling to the ground. Then she swung the hammer down again and hit the second pane of glass on the inside of the door.

All the dogs barked and were watching them through their kennel gates. Wally hopped through the broken door, setting off an alarm. His heart started pounding in his chest. Screeching noises blasted throughout the building, echoing off the tile floors and brick walls. Sarah covered her ears and yelled, "Find Bop!"

Wally jogged down the right side of the kennel room, calling out, "Bop? Bop?"

"Bop?" Sarah shouted into the kennels on the other side.

Wally thought he heard Bop's bark, but he couldn't tell where it came from with the commotion of the alarm and other barking dogs.

They turned right down a short hallway and continued their search. "Bop?" Wally called out. They combed every kennel, but still couldn't find Bop.

"We got Bee Bee down there," Sarah said, pointing at a small hallway back in the direction they came from.

As they ran past the kennel room they had entered from, red and blue flashing lights lit up the trees just outside the door Sarah had broken. Wally ran across the hall to a kennel at the end of the row and shouted, "Here he is!" when he found Bop wagging his tail and jumping in circles.

Wally unfastened the kennel door and Bop squealed as he rushed through the gate, then jumped up onto Wally's shoulders and kissed his face. "Good boy, Bop," Wally said, petting his head.

Sarah tugged on Wally's shirt, "Let's get out of here." She was holding something in her other hand, but Wally couldn't tell what.

They broke into a sprint and turned the corner back into the kennel room they entered through. A deep voice boomed from just inside the doorway. "What the hell? What are you kids doing in here?!" the man exclaimed.

Wally dropped to the ground and used his right middle and ring fingers to depress the button of the canister strapped to his forearm, spraying silly string at the man. Flashing police lights from the car outside lit up the left half of the man's body. It was a cop! He was large and breathed heavily as he swiped at the silly spray. "Stop right there and I'll take you home," he said, stepping toward them.

Sarah raised the Snow in a Can out in front of her and shouted, "It's the popo!" She pressed down on the button. White foam shot out of the canister toward the cop, hitting him in the eyes.

"Ahh!" the cop screamed. He covered his face and turned to run the other way, but tripped and fell.

Sarah held the button down and ran closer, spraying toxic snow onto the side of the cop's face. "Stop. Stop!" he shouted, curling into the fetal position.

Wally and Bop jumped through the broken door and ran outside.

"Leave us alone," Sarah yelled, then she jumped through the door and followed.

Wally, Sarah, and Bop ran through the parking lots of business complexes and warehouses until they reached the Creek Path that ran along Boulder Creek. Cop cars flashing their lights sped down the street heading in the direction of the Humane Society.

Wally unclipped the magic leash and collar from his shoulder and fastened them onto Bop. Bop sat down and barked. "Ruff!"

"Shh," Wally told him, "we still have to make it home."

"Ask him about the meaning of life," Sarah told him.

Wally hugged Bop, then pulled away and asked the dog, "Bop, can you tell us the meaning of life so my dad can be happy?"

Bop looked up at Wally panting, then licked his nose. Wally dropped his head. He knew Bop didn't know how to talk.

"Maybe he needs to be bribed," Sarah suggested.

"He seems pretty nice," Wally responded.

"I'm nice too, but sometimes I make my dad bribe me," Sarah explained. "We could take him to get ice cream?"

Wally reached his hand in his pocket, "I still have the hundred dollars," he said, holding the crumpled bill up.

Sarah pulled out her dad's phone and said, "Siri, take us to get ice cream."

Siri responded, "Ripple Frozen Yogurt is 2.5 miles away. Would you like me to route you there?"

"Yes," Sarah replied.

"My dad and I love Ripple," Wally said.

Wally, Bop, and Sarah jogged down the Creek Path in the darkness following Siri's directions. Under one of the bridges, they ran past a group of people lounging in a circle. Pendle sat with them, cradling the pitcher of Chocolate Fire, which was nearly empty, and waved at them as they passed. "The magic leash worked!" he shouted. "Now let him teach you all the secrets of the universe."

Wally smiled and waved at Pendle, wondering how he knew things other adults didn't. When they exited the cover of the bridge, Wally turned his attention back on the path, placing his steps carefully as they continued down the icy sidewalk.

Sarah and Wally were both winded by the time they turned off the Creek Path onto a back road. A cop car sped down the cross street in front of them, starling Wally. He dove behind a bush.

Sarah crouched down beside him. "Are they still looking for us?" she asked.

"Probably," Wally whispered. "You made that cop cry."

Wally and Sarah stood back up when the cop turned out of sight. As they walked through a dark parking lot, the illuminated red Ripple sign lit up in the distance and guided the final leg of their journey. There were a few people inside and they all turned and stared at Wally, Sarah, and Bop when they swung the door open and entered wearing their ski masks.

"Welcome to Ripple," a pimply kid with lanky arms said from behind the counter. "Fill your bowl up and come weigh it here to checkout."

Wally grabbed three cardboard bowls and handed one to Sarah. Sarah went straight to the strawberry flavor dispenser and filled her cup until a giant spiraled pile rose above the rim. Then she poured chocolate sauce on top and covered it with rainbow sprinkles. She set her bowl down on the scale at the counter before Wally had even decided on a flavor.

"Get Bop peanut butter," Sarah hollered at him. "It's Bee Bee's favorite."

Wally followed her instructions and filled Bop's cup up with peanut butter frozen yogurt. He went around to several machines and added a little bit of seven different flavors to his bowl, including eggnog, honey baked ham, and Christmas cookie batter. He didn't top his bowl or Bop's with anything.

"That'll be fourteen dollars and sixty-two cents," the kid behind the counter said after Wally placed their bowls on the scale with Sarah's.

Wally handed the teenager the hundred dollar bill. He held the bill up to the light, inspecting it, then slid it under the drawer and counted out the change. Wally shoved the bills and coins into his pocket.

"Let's sit over here," Sarah said.

They sat down inside and removed their masks. Wally ate a few bites of his ice cream before turning to Bop. The dog was lying down with his head cocked and pointed up at them. His eyes were glued on Wally's bowl. "Here, have some of yours," Wally said. He used a small plastic spoon to scoop a big bite of peanut butter frozen yogurt from the bowl and lowered it to Bop's face. Bop licked the spoon furiously until it was shiny and clean.

"I told you he'd like it," Sarah said.

Wally turned back to his bowl and ate a few more bites.

"Eight dollars for an ice cream?!" Wally heard a familiar voice holler from the direction of the cash register. "You won't believe this, but I remember paying a quarter for a scoop just like this."

Wally turned his head to look at who it was. A man with scraggly gray hair and boney legs sticking through baggy shorts faced the register. "Mr. Norris," Sarah whispered. "What should we do?"

Wally turned back the other way and ducked his head, hoping Mr. Norris wouldn't notice them. When he heard the tapping of Mr. Norris's boots approaching, Wally thought back to Mrs. Brenda hunting him in the bathroom stall. His stomach tightened into a knot.

Mr. Norris stopped as he walked past. "Hey, what are you kids doing here?" he asked. "I saw you sold that pitcher to Pendy or whatever the hell that nut's name is."

Red and blue lights reflected off the buildings outside, then a cop car squealed to a stop in front of the frozen yogurt shop.

Wally grabbed Bop's leash and stood up. Sarah pulled something from her backpack and slowly slid out of her seat behind Mr. Norris.

Mr. Norris was holding a large bowl overflowing with hot chocolate frozen yogurt and topped with chunks of Snickers bars. "You know, it's not safe for you to be talking to the likes of that fella. Where are your parents, anyway?" he asked.

A cop ran through the door and held a radio up to his mouth. "Found 'em. Ripple Ice Cream." He was tall and muscular, unlike the last one, and had a boney face and a thick black beard. He waved at Wally and smiled as he slowly approached.

Sarah shouted to Wally, "Run!"

Wally looked up at Mr. Norris's stunned face before turning toward the back door exit.

"Stop!" the cop shouted.

Wally leaned forward and tried to take a step, but a hand grabbed the hood of his jacket. "I knew you kids weren't supposed to be out," Mr. Norris spat. "Your damn parents are so incompetent, it's pathetic."

Wally turned around and saw Sarah charging Mr. Norris like she'd charged her sister, only this time she held Bee Bee's blue dragon toy with both arms like a battering ram and shoved it into Mr. Norris's rear end.

"Ahh!" Mr. Norris cried. He let go of Wally and turned around to see what had struck him.

Sarah turned and ran in the direction of the cop, but Mr. Norris reached down and seized her left arm.

Wally nocked an arrow, pulled the string back, and released. It flew over Mr. Norris's head and struck the cop right between the eyes. The cop stumbled into the tables and fell over a chair.

"I'm coming in," he heard someone say through the cop's radio.

Sarah jerked and flailed, but couldn't escape Mr. Norris's grip. Wally nocked his final arrow and aimed it at Mr. Norris.

"Stranger danger!" Sarah shouted. She swung the dragon toy like a bat, striking Mr. Norris across the face. His head twisted upon impact, the smack echoing throughout the frozen yogurt shop. He dropped his bowl of frozen yogurt and fell to his knees with both hands covering his face. Chunks of Snickers bars scattered on the ground.

"Go!" Sarah yelled again.

Wally saw a second cop approaching the building. He let his final arrow fly just as the officer rushed through the door. The arrow struck him on the cheek with a thunk. He fell sideways into the cash register, knocking a plastic display full of cookies into the pimply teenager.

As Wally turned to run, he saw Sarah bolt toward the door the cops had entered through, wielding the dragon toy like a sword. The first cop rose to all fours and lunged at her as she ran past, but she easily jumped over his arms. The last thing Wally saw as he and Bop fled the frozen yogurt shop was the second cop crawling out from behind the cash register to block the doorway Sarah was charging toward.

CHAPTER 14

WALL-E

WALLY RAN up the stairs of the green apartment complex he and his dad lived in. Bop followed, but limped up each step. When they reached the third floor landing, Bop held his front right paw up and licked it. Wally led them down a hallway and crept up to his front door. "Almost there," he told Bop.

Wally put his ear to the door and listened. His dad was talking, but he couldn't make out any words. He grabbed the handle and turned it slowly. The door slid out of the frame and opened just wide enough for Wally to see inside. His dad was pacing back and forth with his phone pressed against his ear. He was wearing sweatpants and his black puffy jacket. The bags under his eyes were darker than normal and his skin looked pale.

"They were trying to find the meaning of what?" Wally's dad asked. "He said I said that?"

Wally inched back from the door, but kept watching. His dad didn't seem happy he was trying to help.

"Where are they?" he asked. He raised his hand up to his head and ran his fingers through his long, thinning hair. "Did she say where they were going? How did they outrun the cops?"

Bop stuck his nose through the door. Wally tried to use the leash to pull him back, but Bop was too strong. He barked into the room at Wally's dad, "Ruff!"

Wally's heart raced as his father fell silent. He wasn't sure if he should go inside or run. Bop started wagging his tail and pulled himself through the doorway, swinging the door open. Wally was exposed. His dad ran over to him and wrapped him in a hug, "Oh, Buddy, I'm so glad you're safe."

Wally's father crouched down to his eye level, but released his squeeze and pushed the phone back up to his ear. "Sam, he's here." Tears fell from his dad's face. "He's safe, don't worry... Alright, we'll see you tomorrow."

Wally's dad hung up the phone and slipped it into his jacket pocket. Bop jumped onto his shoulders and started licking the tears from his cheeks. Wally's dad laughed, which helped Wally relax. Maybe his dad wouldn't be mad.

Wally's father rubbed Bop's ears. "You're a sweet fella," he said. "I heard you've been on quite the adventure?"

Wally nodded.

"Mr. Evans said you were looking for something? Something for me?" he asked.

Wally bent down and wrapped his arm around Bop's neck. "We were finding the meaning of life because you were really sad that you didn't know so I wanted to get it for you for Christmas."

Wally's dad covered his mouth with his hand, then scrunched his eyes and cried more. "You've got such a good heart... I'm so sorry, Wally."

Wally collided into his dad and gave him a hug. He was happy to be home. He felt his dad's tears hit the side of his neck.

When Wally decided to pull away, his father closed his eyes and took a deep breath, then addressed Wally again. "And who is this guy?" he asked, scratching the top of Bop's head.

"Bop," Wally said.

"Where did you get him?"

"From the Humane Society. Lenny's parents got rid of him."

His dad rested his hand on Wally's shoulder. "I see. And why did you rescue him? It has something to do with me?"

"He knows the meaning of life," Wally stated.

Wally's dad chuckled. "And who taught you that?"

"Mr. Evans," Wally said. "And Lenny told us Bop could talk."

"Of course it was Sam!" His dad laughed louder this time. "Well, thank you for taking care of me."

Bop lifted his paw to his face and licked it again. Wally's dad reached down for Bop's leg. "Oh, what's happened?" he said. He tilted his head and raised Bop's leg in the air to look at the bottom of his foot. One of the pads was bloody and had a piece of glass stuck in it.

Wally's father rushed to the sink and returned with two paper towels, one wet and one dry. "How'd you get this, Buddy?" he asked. He pulled on the piece of glass, but Bop tugged his leg away and whimpered. "Can you help me?" Wally's father asked. "Tell him we aren't going to hurt him and that he'll feel better soon."

Wally stroked Bop's head, "It's going to be OK," he told Bop. Wally's dad grabbed Bop's paw and yanked the piece of glass from his foot. Bop whimpered again, but gave Wally's dad a kiss. They wiped the cut with the wet paper towel, which made it bleed more.

His father handed him the dry paper towel. "Here, press this against his paw," he said. Wally did as his father instructed. Bop flinched a few times from discomfort, but held his paw in the air for Wally.

Wally's dad disappeared into his bedroom for a minute and came back with a roll of white athletic tape. "We'll have to take him to the vet tomorrow. This should do for tonight."

Wally held Bop's paw as his dad wrapped it with the tape. "Have you had anything for dinner?" his father asked.

"We had some ice cream," Wally replied.

His father laughed. "That's not dinner. We have some left-over pizza I could warm up?"

Wally nodded. "Bop likes pizza, too."

"I'm not sure dog's are supposed to eat pizza. Let me cook him up some eggs."

Wally's living room was cluttered with boxes of books, but devoid of any decorations other than the bare Christmas tree with no presents under it. The expanse of empty, white wall was broken up only by a large TV mounted in the corner of the room. Wally sat down on their purple cloth couch. Bop followed him up and lay with his head resting on Wally's criss-crossed legs. He petted Bop while his dad made them dinner.

The soft rumble of Bop's snores started to lull Wally to sleep just as his dad approached with a plate of pizza in one hand and a bowl of scrambled eggs in the other. "Here it is," he said. He handed Wally the plate of pizza and hovered the bowl of steaming scrambled eggs under Bop's nose. Bop's head jerked up and his eye cranked open. He stuck his nose into the bowl and ate laying down on Wally's lap. "I guess I'll stand here and hold it," Wally's dad said laughing.

Wally rested his plate in his lap. "Dad?" he asked.

His dad glanced up at him while holding the bowl as Bop licked the edges clean. "Yes, Wally?"

"Do you want a mom for me?"

His father tilted his head, "Why do you ask that?"

"So you don't have to do two jobs. Mr. Evans thinks Principal Anderson looks like an elf, and Sarah said she isn't married and that she could be my new mom," Wally explained.

"Ha!" Wally's dad laughed. "I love getting to do both jobs. And I don't think I'm Principal Anderson's type."

Wally waited for his father to stop laughing, then asked, "What happened to my mom?"

His dad placed Bop's empty bowl on the coffee table and sat next to him on the couch. He wrapped his arm around Wally as he replied, "She got very sick and died when you were a baby, remember?"

"But how?" Wally asked.

Wally's dad pulled his bottom lip into his mouth, "I want nothing more than to stay around and be your father. If you want to hear what happened to your mother, I'll tell you. But it's a sad story and I don't think it'll make you feel better."

"I want to know," Wally said.

"OK..." his father replied. He paused for a moment and took a deep breath, then continued, "After your mother had you, she had what's called depression. It's where you get very sad and you can't help it and it's hard to feel happy no matter how happy your life is." Wally's father started to breathe faster and his eyes turned red. "Doctors don't know why this happens, but when it does sometimes people...do things they don't want."

"It's like an evil spell?" Wally asked.

His father grinned briefly, but his mouth straightened again when he continued talking, "Yes, it's a very evil spell. One day your mother got so sad she..." His father looked down and considered his words. "She... She decided that...she didn't want to live anymore and she died," he said between gasps.

Wally's face scrunched up when he saw the pain in his father's eyes. "Was it because of me?" he asked.

His father pulled Wally's head into his chest and squeezed him, "No. No. You can never think that," his father cried. "Never say that." His convulsing sobs rocked them back and forth. "She loved us very much, and I know she wanted to be here to see you grow up." Wally pushed his face into his dad's chest. "I know you're scared that I'm sick now too, but I'm not going anywhere," he told Wally. "I promise, I'm not going to leave you." Wally clutched the back of his father's jacket with both hands. Sarah was right. His dad was sick.

After a few moments of relative silence, Bop wedged

himself between Wally and his father, then wiggled his snout up to meet their faces. Wally felt warm air sniffing his ear, then a rough tongue slide across his chin. When Wally pulled away from his father, Bop changed course and went for his dad's face. His father put his hands up to shield himself, but Bop found all the gaps in his limbs and fingers to lick through. Both Wally and his dad started laughing.

Bop pulled away and Wally's dad looked at him. "Have I ever told you where you got your name?" he asked.

Wally shook his head.

His father rose and walked over to a box full of DVD cases with faded colors, wiping his eyes and nose on the way. He knelt down and pulled a movie from the bottom of the box and held it up for Wally to see. "This was your mom's favorite. The robot's name is Wall-e and he saves Earth."

"Can we watch it?" Wally asked.

His father stared at him for a moment, then replied, "Ya, I think we can do that."

Wally's dad cooked a bag of popcorn in the microwave, inserted the movie into the TV, and turned off the lights. Bop curled back up on Wally's lap and his dad sat next to him holding a bowl of buttery popcorn.

His father held the remote up and turned to smile at Wally, "Ready?"

"Do you think we'll ever find the meaning of life?" Wally asked.

His father lowered the remote and looked at him, "You and Bop helped me find it tonight."

Wally's eyes widened, "We did?"

"Yes," his father replied, "I've found everything I was looking for and I'm not sad anymore."

Wally smiled at his dad, then dunked his hand into the bowl of popcorn and stuffed his mouth full as he stroked Bop's head. His dad pressed play and the screen lit up with an animation of outer space.

CHAPTER 15

THE MEANING OF LIFE

ON CHRISTMAS MORNING Wally woke up to the sound of scraping against the wall between his room and his father's. Bop perked his ears and he growled.

"It's OK, Bop," Wally assured him.

Wally and Bop emerged into the hallway and saw his dad stumble out of his bedroom wearing a fake beard and holding a large, foam axe. "Have you seen my shield?" he asked Wally.

Wally shook his head. "What are you doing?"

"We're going over to the Evanses' house, remember?"

Wally didn't know that was their plan, but he bolted into his room without question and threw on his green sweater and a pair of sweatpants. Bop's magic collar rested on his night-stand. After they had finished watching *Wall-e* the night before, Wally's dad had fastened one of his professor bowties onto Bop's neck and told him that Bop was his Christmas present from Santa. The bow was red and covered with white snowflakes.

"Here, Bop," Wally called.

Bop trotted to him and sat as Wally fastened his collar underneath the bowtie, then spun the bow so that it rested on the top of his neck.

On the car ride to the Evanses' house, Wally worried that Sarah had gotten in trouble. What if Santa didn't come for her?

When they arrived, Wally's dad knocked gently on the front door, then entered before anyone answered it.

Wally and Bop pushed their way through the doorway. "Hey, come on in!" Mr. Evans called from the kitchen.

Bee Bee barreled toward Bop, then stopped a few feet short and raised her butt into the air and barked, "Ruff!"

Bop spun in a circle, then lunged toward Bee Bee, yanking Wally's arm when his weight hit the end of the leash. Wally stumbled forward, but held onto the leash. Bop and Bee Bee took turns sniffing each other while wagging their tails. Bee Bee tried to tackle Bop and they began wrestling.

Wally managed to unclip Bop's leash when Bop stood up and Bee Bee ran the other direction. Sarah descended from the staircase as Bop and Bee Bee rammed each other into the wall on their way out the doggy door that opened into the backyard.

"I like his bow," Sarah said to Wally. She was still wearing her glittery sweater with a Menorah on it, but also had a Santa hat resting atop her head.

"My dad said Santa brought us Bop."

Sarah's eyes widened, "He gave me all the *Boxcar Children* books!" she exclaimed, "And seven pairs of underwear."

"Did you get in trouble?"

"My dad was mad, but when I cried and said I was sad that my mom was gone for so long, they forgave me."

The unmistakable scent of butter cooking sweetened dough rushed into Wally's nose. He turned around to inspect the kitchen. Mr. Evans was wearing his cape again. He and Wally's dad patted each other on the back as Mr. Evans pulled a waffle from a steaming iron with a fork.

Wally skated in his socks across the hardwood floor into the kitchen with a smile stretching across his face. "Waffles!" he shouted.

Mr. Evans opened the oven door and pulled out a plate piled high with golden brown waffles. "Everything's ready if you guys are?" he asked Wally's dad.

"Sam, those smell amazing," his father replied.

Eileen was sitting on her mom's lap at the kitchen table tracking the plate of waffles with unblinking eyes. When Mr. Evans set the platter down, Eileen called out, "Mine!" squirming from Mrs. Evans's grip and crawling onto the table.

Mrs. Evans pulled her back into her lap. "You have to share," she said.

Bee Bee and Bop were panting when they came inside. Bop followed Bee Bee into the mud room and Wally heard them take turns slurping water from Bee Bee's bowl.

Wally and Sarah chose seats at the table next to each other. Wally noticed his dad was still smiling as he sat next to Mr. Evans on the other side. It seemed like his father hadn't stopped smiling since they curled up on the couch to watch *Wall-e* the night before. Wally couldn't remember the last time his father had been happy that long. His gift was a success.

Mr. Evans leaned over the table and dropped a waffle on his plate, then another on Sarah's plate. Wally grabbed the maple syrup from the middle of the table and covered his waffle, then passed the jug to Sarah. His mouth watered.

Bop trotted out of the mud room and lay down under Wally's chair, resting his head on Wally's feet.

Sarah and Wally both shoved large bites of waffle into their mouths. The butter- and syrup-saturated waffle made the corners of his mouth broaden into a grin. Sarah leaned over to Wally and asked through a full mouth, "Did Bop tell you the meaning of life?"

Wally nodded his head.

"What was it?" she asked.

"We watched a movie on the couch and ate popcorn."

Sarah's attention shifted back onto her plate as Wally set down his fork. He scanned the table and watched his dad laugh repeatedly at everything Mr. and Mrs. Evans said. Eileen eyed him as she shoved an entire strip of bacon into her mouth. He glanced at Sarah and she smiled back with partially chewed waffle covering her teeth.

Wally tore off a piece of waffle and snuck onto the floor under the table. He scratched Bop's head between his ears until his eyes cracked open, holding the waffle in front of his nose with his other hand. Bop sniffed the breakfast treat, gingerly pulled it from Wally's hand, then swallowed without chewing. He nuzzled Wally's cheek with his whiskers and licked him on the lips.

Wally leaned over and whispered into Bop's ear, "Thank you."

AFTERWORD

Wally and the Holiday Jailbreak is my second published work, closely following a collection of short stories titled, *Tales of Twilight*. I wrote the first few chapters (originally titled *Wally)* in the autumn of 2021. At the time, my wife, dog, and I were living nomadically in Europe. Between responsibilities from my day job and the work of physically moving around, I didn't find enough time to finish before the holiday season and decided to put the project on hold with the hopes of publishing it in time for the holidays the following year.

In between these two holiday seasons, I wrote and posted several short stories on my website that would ultimately be published in the *Tales of Twilight* collection. As I made final revisions to *Tales of Twilight* with my editor, she pointed out that there was a recurring theme of death in my stories. Upon reflection, I realized that not only was she correct, but the stories were more serious in nature than I had intended.

I don't believe that every story needs to be an uplifting fantasy. Hemingway is one of my favorite authors and he certainly wrote with a mournful tone. I've always loved how honest (to use his own word) his writing is, and I think my admiration for him caused me to veer a little too hard down the melancholy path.

I consider myself to be a goofy person with a knack for comedy, and while the honest, sorrowful tone Hemingway mastered does fit my personality to some degree, I realized that I needed to introduce humor into my stories to more accurately reflect and express myself.

When the time came in autumn 2022 where I had to get back to work on *Wally* if I wanted to finish in time for the holiday season, I decided to morph my grim outline about a young boy forced to become an adult before his time as a result of living with his depressed and critically ill father into a comedy. As the story unfolded, *Wally* morphed into *Wally and the Holiday Jailbreak*.

I know my sense of humor leans on the boyish side with plenty of toilet and sex-related jokes, but I did my best to add at least a little something for everyone. There is a ten-year-old child that still lives inside of me and loves to be unleashed.

I didn't have any specific inspiration for *Wally and the Holiday Jailbreak*. Whenever I start a new story, I begin with my characters. Then I put them into a situation and uncover how I think they would react, step by step. The setting in my hometown of Boulder, Colorado may have been my subconscious self expressing its homesickness while we spent the holidays in Europe, far from family and friends. The characters were not modeled off of people I know, nor were their experiences things that have happened to me or anyone I know. When I sat down to write, *Wally and the Holiday Jailbreak* was simply the ink that I left on the paper.

I'm a new writer and the publication of *Wally and the Holiday Jailbreak* marked a significant milestone on my journey. After two years of writing with the intention to publish (and many more before that as a casual hobby), I feel like I'm finally on the cusp of finding my voice. While the reality is probably that "finding your voice" is a moving target authors chase over the course of a lifetime, I'm becoming more confident in claiming my work as "my writing" rather than a blended imitation of writers I admire. Stories are beginning to flow out of me and each word I write feels natural.

This begs the perennial question: what's next? To be honest, as I type these final words, I don't know what I'll work on next. I have several projects with a completed outline and a few first-draft chapters. One is a historical fiction that follows a group of WWII veterans who attempt to be the first people to summit K2; another is thriller that follows a vigilante hacker; and who knows, maybe I'll end up writing a sequel to *Wally and the Holiday Jailbreak*. My plan at the time of writing is to relax during the holidays and do whatever feels most organic at the start of the new year.

Before I started down the path of self-publishing, I would have never picked up a book with zero ratings. Now I understand how daunting it feels to get that first review not written by your wife or mother. If you have time to share your experience and feedback, ratings and reviews on Amazon and

Goodreads can make a huge difference for indie authors like myself.

For an up-to-date list of my published books and a summary of my upcoming work, visit zackthoutt.com/writing/bibliography/.

If you're interested in following my future work, I have a newsletter and reader group called The Storied Scrolls that you can subscribe to on my website (zackthoutt.com). Members receive updates when I publish new stories, earn free content, and have the opportunity to contribute to the development of my books as beta readers.

Enjoy the journey,
Zack

ACKNOWLEDGMENTS

Thank you to my wife, Shelby, for putting up with me staring at a computer all day for work, then staring at a computer in my free time to write.

Thank you to my dog, Skutull, for showing me unconditional love and inspiring Bop's yarn ball scene.

Thank you to my family and friends, for supporting my varied pursuits and encouraging me to follow my dreams.

Thank you to Adele Jordan, my developmental editor and writing mentor, for teaching me how to structure a story and engage readers.

Thank you to Brooks Becker, my copy editor, for preparing the book for publication and teaching me the difference between "smart" and "dumb" quotes.

Thank you to Nicole Britton, my audiobook narrator, for bringing my characters to life and rocking the fart noises.

Thank you to my early readers, for encouraging me and joining me on my writing journey.

Thank you to Santa Claus, who delivered many wonderful gifts over the years. I wish I could say that the best gift he ever gave me was a book series that inspired me to start writing my own stories, but if I'm being honest, it was an Xbox 360. This year I'm asking for the meaning of life.

Author Profile

Zack Thoutt is the author of *Wally and the Holiday Jailbreak*, *Tales of Twilight*, and *Nomad Life*. He posts chapters of his books on his website, zackthoutt.com, where he also runs a reader club and newsletter called The Storied Scrolls.

Zack is the CPO at AutoSalesVelocity, where they build enterprise software for the auto industry. He graduated *summa cum laude* from The University of Colorado Boulder with an engineering degree in applied math.

When Zack isn't at his computer writing stories or software, he's typically in the kitchen experimenting with new recipes, playing board games with friends, or traveling with his wife, Shelby, and their dog, Skutull.

Made in the USA
Middletown, DE
15 December 2022

18661627R00083